Brave Dave
And
The Caribbean Conspiracy

By
Simon Woodward
Illustrated by Ralph Platt

This book is copyright. Subject to statutory exception and to provisions of relevant collective licensing agreements, no part of this publication may be reproduced without the prior written permission of the author.

In this work of fiction, the characters, the places and events are either the product of the author's imagination or they are used entirely fictitiously. Any resemblance to actual persons, sentient beings, living or dead is purely coincidental.

For Molly and Tilly, my daughters

As with each of the stories in the Brave Dave series there are numerous people I have to thank for their help and assistance. But especially for *The Caribbean Conspiracy*, I must thank; Chris and John Debenham, Yve my wonderful wife, Peter Robinson, Dave Judd, Sophie Evans and last but not least Mark Allen. All that said, Brave Dave and the characters he meets would never have happened if it wasn't for the series illustrator, Ralph Platt.

Chapter 1. A Muddy Pen _____ *1*

Chapter 2. Time for a Rest _____ *5*

Chapter 3. Inventing _____ *11*

Chapter 4. The Ultimate Random Holiday Picker _____ *17*

Chapter 5. Flying Bricks _____ *33*

Chapter 6. A Holiday _____ *35*

Chapter 7. Land Lords and Scarper _____ *39*

Chapter 8. Sprouts _____ *57*

Chapter 9. Transport _____ *61*

Chapter 10. Trolleys _____ *65*

Chapter 11. Flying Luggage _____ *73*

Chapter 12. Five Sense and Some _____ *91*

Chapter 13. The Announcement _____ *95*

Chapter 14. 10,000ft is Quite High Up _____ *99*

Chapter 15. Mince Pies _____ *109*

Chapter 16. Landing and TAP _____ *113*

Chapter 17. Gilbert Bates _____ *125*

Chapter 18. Holiday Home _____ *131*

Chapter 19. My Little Rat _____ *135*

Chapter 20. Perception is Nine Tenths of the Look__ 145

Chapter 21. Pedalo Power _____ *155*

Chapter 22. Wrapping Entertainment _____ *169*

Chapter 23. A Pay Rise! _____ *173*

Chapter 24. Displays and Swizzle Sticks _____ *179*

Chapter 25. The Evil Doers' Dastardly Plan _____ *195*

Chapter 26. EV1L-5A/NTA _____ *201*

Chapter 27. Flip-Flops and Pink Sunglasses _____ *209*

Chapter 28. A Delivery _____ *231*

Chapter 29. Bobboggs and Bungle-bees _____ *235*

Chapter 30. Robot Flat Packs _____ *245*

Chapter 31. Stiff Legs and Evil Beach Bags _____ *253*

Chapter 32. A Floppy Hat and Nice Tights _____ *265*

Chapter 33. Lettuce Custard and Mobile Phones ___ *293*

Chapter 34. Text Message Rules _____ *297*

Chapter 35. Hot Stuff _____ *307*

Chapter 36. No More Buttons _____ *313*

Chapter 37. Santa is Free _____ *317*

Chapter 38. End of the Holiday _____ *329*

Chapter 39. Back Home _____ *341*

About the Author _____ *347*

Chapter 1.
A Muddy Pen

Tariq and Dave let go of Jonesy's claws, dropped to the ground and landed in Tariq's muddy pen. Jonesy squawked his farewells and flew off to find his swans.

It was early November and the evening was drawing in. For Tariq to be up this time of year was very unusual as he was a tortoise; a gifted tortoise, if you asked him, and an insomniac one at that. His friend was Dave, a particularly unusual feather, being one who walked and talked and wore an interesting feather-tight, yellow Lycra bodysuit.

Both of them had met up when Jonesy, another unusual individual, had shed Dave whilst taking a flock of Mute Swans south for the winter during a huge lightning storm a few weeks previously. This alone was peculiar because Mute Swans don't migrate and Jonesy was a buzzard anyway.

However, the circumstances around Dave and Tariq's meeting never struck either of them as particularly strange and they had become close friends.

Apart from Dave's close call with a wannabe poltergeist, Dave and Tariq had worked together to solve a mystery involving a small magical being called a Time Goblin.

Chapter 2.
Time for a Rest

Dave and Tariq made their way from the end of Tariq's pen to his hutch.

"I'm glad to be home," said Tariq.

"I'm glad to be back at your hutch," Dave said. "Don't know where I should go now though," he finished, a little downhearted that their adventures together had come to an end.

"Dave. Stay here," Tariq said. "I've got plenty of room."

"I couldn't impose," said Dave, very conscious of the fact that he had just turned up, some weeks ago, and had been accepted by Tariq without even asking — almost.

"Dave," Tariq began, "in the short time I've known you, you've done good and great deeds for people you didn't even know. I would like to be part of that, if you'll let me."

Dave was touched by Tariq's sentiment. "Okay. Thanks Tariq, I'll take you up on your offer then."

"Tremendous," said Tariq, opening the door to his hutch, indicating for Dave to go in. "Okay. What's the plan of action?" Tariq continued as he put the kettle on for a well-deserved cup of tea.

"None," said Dave. "I think we need a break, a holiday — just something."

"I believe you're right," Tariq agreed. He hadn't been on holiday before. "Where shall we go then?"

"Don't know. You choose Tariq," Dave said.

"I couldn't. You choose. You've done all the work. It must be your choice," Tariq answered.

"No, I can't possibly. You choose," Dave continued.

"No, no, Dave, you choose. Go on," said Tariq.

"Are you sure?"

"Yes, yes." Tariq said.

"I couldn't. You choose," Dave said again.

"Oh, just get on with it," Shell said butting in, getting fed up with the whole conversation.

"Who said that?" Dave asked, looking around wondering whether he had heard someone else say something.

"Er, it was me," Tariq answered. He didn't feel that Dave was ready to find out about Shell yet.

"But your voice Tariq, it was different somehow; higher in fact."

Tariq, clearing his throat and attempting to speak a little higher and more like Shell, said, "Okay, how about neither of us choose and I devise a random method of holiday choice, a bit like the way the balls for the National Lottery are picked. I mean, at the end of the day, I *am* an inventor."

"Tariq why are you talking in that squeaky voice?" Dave questioned, before adding, "Actually I don't want to know, and I suppose you are an inventor of sorts."

"What do you mean, '*of sorts*'? I am an inventor. I have created lettuce soup, I have devised the Concretonator and I have started the most excellent culinary cuisine of lettuce custard."

"Okay. Accepted," Dave conceded. "Now devise the best ever random holiday picker."

"I will," Tariq said. He liked a challenge.

Chapter 3.
Inventing

Tariq walked to the back of his hutch and pulled at an old, grimy rug that was hanging on the back wall. The rug was patterned; although the design had been lost under layers of yucky dirt that had built up over the many winters Tariq had been using it to cover a secret doorway to a secret staircase. Behind the door and down the stairs was Tariq's secret underground laboratory where he did all of his inventing.

At the bottom of the stairs Tariq looked along the shelves that lined the walls of his lab. There were plenty of map books on them, scattered between the other bits and pieces he had collected over the years.

Tariq walked quickly, in a slow fashion as he was a tortoise, around the lab's shelving, picking up the bits he thought he would need to make his random holiday picker. Throwing the parts he needed into the centre of his workshop floor, he continued to trawl around his supplies.

He took map books from the shelves; he took cocktail sticks from them, a food blender, one of those round red squat vacuum cleaners which usually have a face painted on them and are normally called Henry, a dartboard, and finally a large piece of light grey plastic drainpipe.

Tremendous, thought Tariq. He was certain he had picked everything from the shelves he would need to build the ultimate random holiday picker machine.

Tariq got to work on the grey piping and the vacuum cleaner and then called up the stairs to Dave. "Can you come down and give me a hand with this?"

"Okay Tariq," Dave called back and got up from Tariq's sofa, putting down the book he had found on his host's bookshelf.

"That *Who's who of Magical Beings* by the Guild of Gaia is quite an interesting book," Dave said as he walked into Tariq's lab. "What do you need me to do then?"

"Can you get that dartboard?" Tariq said, pointing to the dartboard he had retrieved from his lab's shelving, "and those cocktail sticks," Tariq continued, pointing to the cocktail sticks he'd also pulled from his lab's shelves, "and start sticking the cocktail sticks into the dartboard?"

Dave stared at Tariq agog, in the bemused way Dave usually did at most of Tariq's suggestions. What could he say?

"Okay Tariq. Let me get this clear in my head. You want me to use those cocktail sticks and stick them into that dartboard, and somehow out of all this, you're going to make a random holiday picker?"

"Yep, that's about the long and short of it," Tariq said in a matter-of-fact manner.

Dave picked up the dartboard from the pile of stuff Tariq had pulled from the shelves and placed it on the top of a small workbench then emptied the box of cocktail sticks next to it.

After three hours of exceedingly boring work Dave had stuck every single cocktail stick into the dartboard. All 2,000 of them!

The dartboard now looked like some kind of red, black and yellow hedgehog, one that had been run over by a particularly heavy steamroller, to which some lunatic hairdresser had applied half a tonne of Shock Waves hair gel, leaving it with an incredibly spiky appearance.

"Right Tariq. I'm done," said Dave, relieved his task was complete.

"Good. Hang it on the wall over there," Tariq said, pointing at the back wall of his lab.

Chapter 4.
The Ultimate Random Holiday Picker

The machine was very simple in its design. The food blender fed into the grey piping and the vacuum cleaner had been changed to blow instead of suck; its hose was threaded through a hole in the bottom of the drainpipe. The open end of the drainpipe was pointed at the cocktail stick covered dartboard.

"What happens now?" asked Dave.

"What happens now," Tariq started to explain, "is that I drop these map books into the blender section of the Ultimate Random Holiday Picker and whichever part of whichever map sticks on the cocktail stick sticking out from the centre of the bullseye, is where we will go for our holiday."

"Tariq," started Dave, "you are totally bonkers. Do you know that?"

"No excellent tortoise is free from a mixture of madness and genius," Tariq retorted.

"What's that supposed to mean?" Dave said, frowning.

"I'm not quite sure...but I think it's relevant."

"Okay, whatever," Dave said. "Turn it on then."

Tariq turned on the machine and once it had got up to the right spin level Tariq started dumping the map books into it.

Flup, flup, flup, flip, flip, flip, went the machine.

Bits of paper flew out of the Ultimate Random Holiday Picker at incredible speeds, mainly covering the lab floor, but some bits did stick in the dartboard. None hit the bullseye however. After several long minutes (the ones made out of 120 seconds, rather than the usual 60) Tariq was down to his last map book. It was one of the Caribbean. He carefully fed it into the blender and out came the shredded bits of map, flying through the air.

Flup, flup, flup, flip, flip, flip, went the machine again. The last map book was done.

"Look!" Tariq said to Dave once the machine had finished shredding the last map. "There's one piece of map stuck on the bullseye. What does it say?"

"Turn that machine off and I'll have a look," Dave said, wary of Tariq's inventions; he'd not had good experiences in the past.

Tariq turned the machine off and Dave went to retrieve the single piece of paper that had stuck to the cocktail stick poking from the centre of the dartboard's bullseye.

"What does it say? Where is it?" Tariq questioned.

"It says Maiti and from the look of it, it's in the Caribbean," said Dave.

"Wow," said Tariq and then added, "I've never heard of it."

"Never heard of the Caribbean? It's where Bob comes from."

"No, of course I've heard of the Caribbean... a bit. I mean Maiti."

"Neither have I," Dave agreed.

"Who's Bob?" Tariq asked.

"You must have heard of Bob."

"No. Bob who?"

"Bob the Tail Feather, a legend in his own wingspan," Dave said name dropping. Tariq was still none the wiser. "Don't know about Maiti though," Dave finished, seeing that Tariq had no idea about who he was talking about.

"Don't worry. I'm sure I've got a book on it somewhere," Tariq said, wandering up the stairs back into his hutch. Leaving the doorway from his lab Tariq made straight for the wooden bookshelf that housed his entire library and Dave followed.

Tariq ran his finger across the spine of each book on the shelf hoping to discover one that would tell them where they were going.

"Hmmm," he said, stopping on the third book from the end. "I think this is the one." Tariq pulled the book from the shelf.

"What book is that?" Dave queried.

"It is *The Atlas of Lesser Known Land Masses*," Tariq said quoting from the book's cover. He began thumbing through its index. "Here it is Dave. Apparently this island is only about ten square kilometres in area which, roughly speaking, is only 17 times the size of the Mall in Washington DC, in America."

"What's that in English?" Dave asked.

"About 17 times 146 acres," said Tariq.

"Not that big then, Tariq?"

"No not really. It's also a Cockney colony," Tariq added, reading a little more from the passage in his book.

"You mean its residents are originally from the East End of London?" Dave asked.

"I suppose so," Tariq replied. "The book says that it was 'originally settled by Cockney emigrants from London after the Grate Fire of 1866'."

"I thought the Great Fire was in 1666. That book must be wrong." Dave pointed out.

"No, Dave. The **Grate** Fire of 1866 is a historical turning point in the long history of Tortoise kind. Back in those days we tortoises were quite new to this country and the weather was very cold. It took a most wise tortoise, called Tarquin the Most Wise, to invent a hutch warming apparatus to get around the problem of the cold weather. But there was a problem with his first design. When he started the fire, in his hutch, he expected the grate to stop the burning embers from spilling out onto the floor, which it did very well. What he didn't expect was how well the grate concentrated the fire's heat.

The hutch warmed up very quickly and he was so pleased with the result he decided to immediately write down the details of his invention.

"While his back was turned away from the fire, as he was scribbling his notes in his notebook et cetera, he didn't notice that, although the burning embers were kept in place, the flames weren't.

"He only just got out of the hutch before the whole thing caught alight. This is when tortoise kind made their next great discovery."

"What's that?" Dave said, curious.

"Heat rises!" Tariq said.

Dave rolled his eyes. "He wasn't related to you by any chance?"

Tariq looked at Dave, crossed his arms and smiled, nodding proudly.

Oh my word. Dave thought to himself. "Okay, I accept the Grate Fire of 1866. And *this* is why some Cockney people left London?" Dave asked.

"No, I think that was just a coincidence," Tariq said.

"Does your fascinating book say anything else?" Dave said, not really wanting to know anymore, hoping that the answer would be no.

"Actually, Dave, it does."

Dave sighed inwardly. *There can't be more*, he thought.

"It says," Tariq continued, "'In 1867 the Island of Maiti was made a British protectorate', I think that's something to do with Britain having control over Maiti and offering protection for that control or something like that. 'After that time the British Navy used the island's natural harbours as protection against Caribbean storms'," Tariq quoted from the book. "'The official language is English but they also speak a regional dialect called cockney patois'."

"Is that it, or does your book have any more wonderful details about the Isle of Maiti by any chance?" Dave said, knowing that the last bit Tariq had read out had to be *the* last bit.

"Just one other thing," Tariq began. Hearing this Dave rolled his eyes as his friend continued. "It says that some of the people on the island follow a religion called Yoodoo and the religious leaders of Yoodoo are called houngan, sort of shaman or witch doctors, and they have special powers. According to the book they can tell the future in special ceremonies, a bit like Madam Josie I suppose."

"Witch doctors... Future... Madam Josie... Right! Well that's good to know — wait a minute. Who's Madam Josie?"

"Madam Josie," Tariq explained in a hushed voice, "is a very special person; she lives under a large rhubarb leaf at the bottom of the garden, a few metres from the end of my pen in fact. She's a fortune teller you know."

"What kind of special fortune telling person would live under a rhubarb leaf?" Dave said, astounded by this new revelation.

"Mystic Madam Josie the Snail, nonetheless. She can gaze deeply into the mists of her shell and tell what has been, what is, and what will be."

"Very interesting Tariq but I think it's time to close that book so we can start concentrating on the holiday. The only problem we have now is to work out how we get there."

"Dave, the lettuce is in your vegetable patch, as they say," Tariq said, quoting a well-known tortoise saying. "This was your idea." he finished.

Chapter 5.
Flying Bricks

Normally Dave would just fly to the Isle of Maiti but now he was alone, flight-wise, the rest of his crowd were off with the bird he had been born from, and his remaining friend was a tortoise.

He looked Tariq up and down. It was obvious to him that tortoises were not strictly of an aerodynamic nature, that is, tortoises were of a shape that really didn't work when attempting to fly. A more appropriate word would be brick-like.

Dave nodded to himself. *Yep*, he thought. *Getting Tariq airborne would be the same as trying to get a brick to fly.*

But Tariq couldn't help it, he was a tortoise. There was only one way to get to Maiti and to do that, they had to catch an aeroplane. How they were going to catch a plane, Dave did not know, but one thing was for sure, they would do it...somehow.

Chapter 6.
A Holiday

John and Julie Jones were doing their last minute checks, making sure they had their passports, their two children's passports and anything else they hadn't packed for their holiday yet.

"Are we going now, are we going now?" Maddy said, jumping up and down with glee.

Maddy was the elder of the Jones's two children. She was seven and had shoulder length mousey brown hair, some of which stuck up from her crown pretending to be a natural pony tail of sorts.

"No, no, dear. We're going tomorrow," her mother said, trying to calm Maddy down before bedtime. Their youngest was Jim and only just five years old. The sandy haired child was already in bed asleep with his teddy.

"Come on now Maddy. You've got to go to bed. We have a very early start in the morning," her dad chipped in.

"Oh. But Dad?" Maddy said.

"Come on Maddy, no buts. Off to bed with you," John said.

"But Dad?" Maddy continued.

"Now," her dad said in a tone that meant this was the end of the conversation.

"Oh! Okay." Maddy stomped off to her bedroom.

"John you best go and make sure that the tortoise is still hibernating," Julie said.

"Of course it's still hibernating. It's a tortoise."

"Please John. You know Maddy and Jim will be extremely upset if anything happens to him while we're away. And stop calling it 'it', his name is Tariq and Tariq is Maddy and Jim's most favourite pet in the whole world."

"Okay then. You check the passports," John replied.

John went out to the back garden through the kitchen to check on the tortoise.

Chapter 7.
Land Lords and Scarper

Wow, Wow. Wow, Wow.

"WHAT ON EARTH IS THAT NOISE?" Dave said, trying to yell over the top of a siren that had just started wowing.

Suddenly the sofa Dave had made himself comfortable on for the evening, threw him off as it bounded across the floor towards a hole in the hutch wall, which had apparently appeared from nowhere. "NOW WHAT'S HAPPENING?" Dave continued yelling over the noise of the sirens.

"Dave, this is an emergency. The Land Lords are coming," Tariq said ominously.

Just as Dave was opening his mouth to ask what the Land Lords were, it was suddenly filled with straw that had started to be sprayed from pipes in the ceiling, pipes he hadn't noticed before.

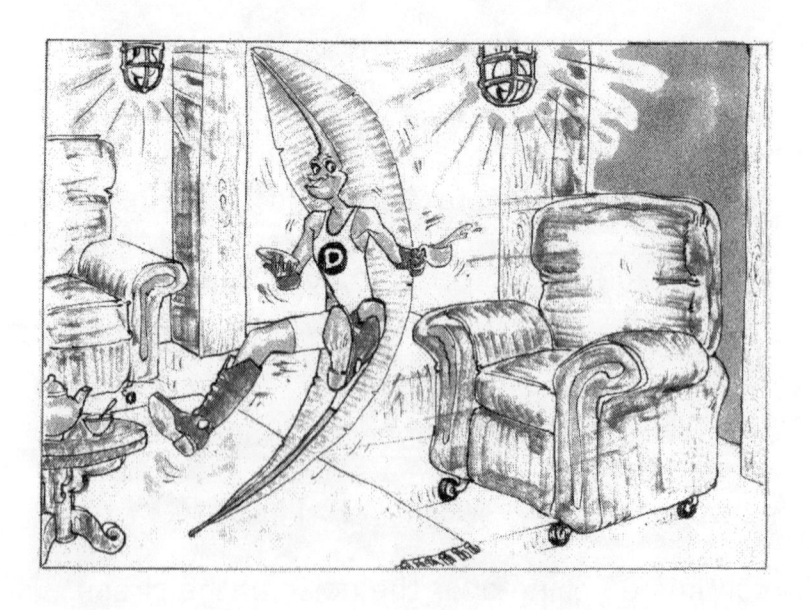

Clawing the straw from his mouth Dave continued to question Tariq. "Where's the sofa gone? What's happened to the rest of the furniture? And what is all this straw for?" He said in a worried tone.

"Dave, the Land Lords are coming," Tariq repeated, adding, "and this place has to look like it is the place of a tortoise who has been, and still is, asleep for the winter, as stated in the contract."

The siren suddenly stopped leaving Dave and Tariq in a completely silent darkness.

"Why?" Dave asked. But before he could say anymore he was interrupted by a low squeaking sound.

"Dave just lie down and make like a feather," Tariq whispered urgently. He disappeared into his shell as fast as he could, bumping his legs as he did so.

"Ouch," Shell uttered.

"Shut up Shell. And be quiet," Tariq said firmly and quietly.

The low squeaking sound continued and starlight gradually seeped through a gap that was appearing in the ceiling as the front half of the hutch roof was lifted up.

"Ooph," said Dave.

BANG!

The roof to the hutch was dropped shut. There was silence and the darkness continued as it had before the roof had been opened.

After a few minutes the inside of the hutch was gradually lit up by some dim red lights.

"Tariq can you get this huge carrot off me?" Dave strained to say as the weight of the large vegetable was making it very hard for him to say anything.

"Okay, I think the coast is clear now," Tariq said.

Tariq popped out of his shell and walked across the room to pull the carrot off Dave, a carrot the Land Lords had kindly thrown into the hutch.

"What was that?" Dave asked.

"That was a carrot Dave. Actually it still is," Tariq said.

"I know that. But what was all that noise and straw about?"

"Ah! That. Tremendous, eh?" Tariq said feeling pleased with himself. "That was S.C.A.R.P.A."

"Scarper? How could I? I had a huge great carrot on me," Dave moaned.

"Not scarper, S.C.A.R.P.A, my siren for Controlled Action and Relative Proximity Alert."

"What?" Dave said utterly dumbfounded by Tariq's answer.

"Basically," Tariq began to explain, "it's a little system I knocked up to sound a siren and let me know I had to do something because the Land Lords were coming. But I do agree with you that is a particularly large carrot."

"You're telling me," Dave said, as he rubbed his bruised stomach.

"That was a close call," Tariq said, wandering over to the wall and pressing a knot in one of the wooden panels that made up the sides of his hutch.

"Hold on tight now Dave."

What now? Dave thought to himself.

All of a sudden a low hissing sound started, gradually increasing in intensity, until it became a very loud hissing sound indeed.

Whilst Dave was looking around the room trying to identify where the sound was coming from, bits of straw, one by one, stood up straight, did a little jig and then leapt from the floor into the pipes that were now sticking out of the ceiling once again. It was as if the straw had come to life and decided to take up one-way trampolining as a profession.

Uh oh, Dave thought, as he decided it would be a good idea to hold tight. Seeing nothing in sight, as the furniture was still hidden away in the walls of the hutch, Dave lunged for Tariq's leg.

Once the hissing sound had reached its maximum noise level the remaining straw got up from the floor and leapt into the pipes above. After five minutes the hissing sound stopped and all the straw in the hutch had gone. Dave let go of Tariq's leg.

"That carrot gives me a great idea Dave," Tariq said as if nothing had happened.

"Tariq, forget the carrot and tell me what just happened here, Okay?" Dave said crossly.

"Dave, keep your hair...... Okay. It's very simple. The Land Lords allow me to live on this plot of land and in return I have agreed to sleep during the winter and eat the food they give during the spring, summer and half of the autumn."

"And that's it?" Dave said.

"Yep, that's about the long and short of it. Tremendous, eh?"

"There's nothing else?"

"Well, not quite nothing else," replied Tariq.

"Well?" Dave questioned, wanting to know more.

"On occasions, during the summer, as it states in the contract," Tariq started to explain, "I have to race next door's rabbit and lose. If I'm asked to that is."

"Lose?" Dave said smiling. "That can't be too difficult."

"That's easy for you to say, but, I bet you didn't know that me and my kind are the fastest animals on earth."

Dave slapped a hand to his mouth to stifle a snigger. "Come off it Tariq, everyone knows tortoises are slow."

"Well that's where you are wrong along with everyone else. Many, many moons ago, a long while before I was born, a long while before my father was born, and a long while before my grandfather was born, and a long while before his father was born, and a long..."

"Okay, I get the idea," Dave interrupted.

"We tortoises made a pact," Tariq continued explaining, "an agreement with Gaia, Mother Nature if you will, that if we kept our speed slow then we would be able to live incredibly long lives, but we had to keep this agreement totally secret."

"And now you've told me," Dave said.

"I know. But you're a good friend and I think that you'll keep this little titbit of information to yourself."

"Of course Tariq, you can trust me. We are friends, good friends aren't we?" Dave said.

"Yes. Of course we are," Tariq replied.

"Okay. I won't tell a soul. How fast can you go?" Dave asked.

"I've already told you too much and this is where I am going to leave it," Tariq said.

"Okay. So the Land Lords make you eat their food and make you sleep."

"Yes."

"So why did the Land Lords come and visit you when, as far as they are concerned, you are asleep?" Dave said.

"I think they were just checking on me before they go to a place called Jamaica, for their holiday."

"Jamaica?" Dave repeated.

"Yeah."

"Jamaica?" Dave repeated once again.

"Yeah," Tariq said, once more, wondering why Dave kept repeating the word Jamaica.

"JAMAICA?" Dave carried on repeating.

"Yeah. Have you gone deaf?" Tariq said frowning.

"No," said Dave. "The Land Lords are going to Jamaica."

"Yeah," Tariq agreed, still frowning.

"Don't you have any idea about what I'm trying to say?"

"Yeah, you're trying to tell me you heard me."

"No. THE LAND LORDS ARE GOING TO JAMAICA," Dave said, quoting Tariq once more.

"Right. Tomorrow. Am I missing something?"

"Do you know where Jamaica is?" Dave asked.

"Not really Dave. But I'm sure I've got a book on it somewhere," Tariq said, without any clue as to what his friend was trying to get at.

"Tariq, it's in the Caribbean," Dave said exasperated.

"Okay. And?" Tariq was still some many millions of miles away from what his friend was trying to say.

"The Caribbean, Tariq," Dave repeated.

"Oh! I think I can see where you're coming from," Tariq said.

"At last," Dave sighed.

"They're going away and during this time we can make our escape from this garden to start our journey towards the Island of Maiti."

"Sort of," Dave said.

"And they won't notice that we've gone because they will have gone as well!" Tariq said finally, now understanding the stance Dave had taken throughout their entire conversation.

"NO," Dave almost shouted. "We can catch a lift."

"So we're going to Jamaica now?" Tariq said.

"No, Maiti is on the way," Dave replied, keeping hold of his annoyance. He knew that on occasions some things just didn't click with Tariq.

"B e c a u s e Jamaica is in the Caribbean!" said Tariq as the penny dropped. He had finally got it.

"Exactly." Dave sighed inwardly. *Sometimes Tariq...Are you really fast*? he thought.

"That means we have to leave tomorrow," Tariq continued.

"Yes."

"We've got lots to do then."

"Yes we have."

"Tremendous," said Tariq.

Chapter 8.
Sprouts

Dave got up exceptionally early the next morning and knocked on Tariq's shell.

"Come on Tariq. Time to get moving. What are you doing in there anyway?"

"Just creating a most excellent new culinary delight for my cook book," Tariq said.

Dave was afraid to ask, but curiosity got the better of him. "What delight is that, dare I ask?"

"Chocolate pudding surprise," Tariq said.

Dave was truly surprised at the answer and this had nothing to do with the pudding. *Was Tariq creating something tasty for a change?* He wondered.

"What's the surprise?" asked Dave.

"It's made from carrot and sprouts. The carrot the Land Lords threw in gave me the idea."

"Okay Tariq, I think we need to get a move on," Dave said, not bothering to make any further comment about Tariq's strange ideas on good food.

It was so early in the morning it was still dark. Tariq had convinced Dave the previous evening that he should take his shell suit, the one created by the Concretonator, just in case.

Dave was still not sure about the whole plan on how to get to Maiti, but the first hurdle was dealt with. They now had a means to get to a plane which was going in the general direction of Maiti.

Tariq and Dave loaded all their luggage into a trolley Tariq had made. The trolley looked like a small open top box with a handle. Dave had his shell suit and Tariq had his satchel, which he had filled with all sorts of stuff from his laboratory, just in case.

After they were packed they sneaked around to the front of the house and pushed the trolley under a stationary growling thing which Dave now knew was a car, something he hadn't known a few weeks earlier. He'd learnt a lot since he had landed in the mud at the end of Tariq's pen on All Hallows Eve.

They fastened the handle of the trolley to the rear bumper of the car with a short piece of rope; then sat in the trolley to wait to be taken to the airport. The sun was not yet above the horizon and it was still quite dark.

Chapter 9.
Transport

John Jones stood outside the children's bedroom door and pushed it open. "Come on kids. Up you get. While you're having breakfast I'll load up the car." John then turned to Julie. "I'll load the car, can you sort out the children?"

John heaved the suitcases down the stairs. When he got to the car he plonked the heavy cases into the boot; then went back inside to have his breakfast.

"Are we going on holiday now?" Maddy mumbled through a mouth full of cereal.

"Yes we are darling," her mum replied. "And try not to speak with your mouthful Maddy; it's disgusting."

"Oh goody," Maddy said, ignoring her mother's plea; then turning to her younger brother she said, "we're going on holiday."

"I want my teddy," Jim replied

"Here you are Jimmy, we haven't forgotten him," Julie said.

"Thanks Mummy," Jim said, grabbing his bear close to his chest.

"Julie, the car's all loaded," John said. "Is everyone ready?" He asked his family.

"Come on kids. Into the car," Julie said, ushering their children towards the front door.

"Yay," said Maddy with glee. This was going to be her first holiday '*a board*', whatever that meant, it was something her Mummy and Daddy had talked about a lot.

Julie and the kids were now seated in the car. John checked the house to make sure it was all secure, one last time, and then got into the car to take everyone to the airport.

Chapter 10.
Trolleys

Dave was roused from his dozing and Tariq peeked out from his shell, when the car they were beneath and attached to, started up with a huge *growl, growl*, as its engine was revved.

"I think we are about to leave," Dave pointed out to Tariq.

"I believe you are right."

"It's probably a good idea to hold tight now Tariq," Dave said.

"Okay. Are you ready?" said Tariq, a little afraid of what was going to happen next.

"I certainly am," said Dave, not really certain that he was.

Dave and Tariq held on to each other whilst trying to hold on to the trolley at the same time. The car lurched forward and before the trolley started to move, the early morning sky was revealed showing twinkling stars, and the freshness of the morning air made them shudder.

All of a sudden the slack in the rope, which tied their trolley to the car, was taken up, and they were jerked off the Jones's driveway very fast, both of them sliding to the back of the trolley only just managing to hold on.

The car motored steadily down the road and the intrepid couple of holidaymakers, Dave the Feather and Tremendous Tariq the Tortoise, held on tight in the dawn twilight. As they were dragged behind the car, the hard little plastic wheels of the trolley made them feel every single bump in the road's surface. Their teeth chattered as if they were freezing cold. And when they hit pot holes their trolley bounced up and down, left and right. It was all very alarming and when it happened, it was all they could do to hold on to one another and the trolley.

Eventually the car reached the main road and when it did it began to speed up, and all they could see of the grass verge was a green and brown blur flashing past them. Dave began to wonder whether his great idea was that great after all.

Finally the car began to slow down and an orange light on the back of the car started to blink in an orange colour. The car turned right and a few moments later it came to a halt in the airport car park. Before the Jones's got out of their car, Tariq and Dave pushed the trolley back under it. They both looked at each other and quietly agreed that travelling in this style was not something they wanted to do again, ever.

*

John Jones emptied the boot and put all their luggage onto a trolley that Julie had picked up from the airport's trolley park.

"I'm glad that we could fly from the local airport," John said to his wife.

"Yes, it makes sense. The journey is better for the kids, particularly as the flight is going to be so long," she replied.

The flight was due to take off at 7.30am, the Jones family had arrived a good two hours before it was due to leave.

In the past John and Julie had had many problems identifying their luggage when they had arrived at their holiday destination, as everyone always seemed to use the same suitcases as them. To get around this problem John had bought some new and distinctive suitcases, ones that would be easily recognisable, so they would never have a problem picking out their cases ever again.

The Jones's suitcases were unique; each and every one, all two of them, had a large Union Jack painted on either side.

Once the car was locked up the Jones family made their way to the departure lounge with their luggage trolley.

Chapter 11.
Flying Luggage

"W w w w what do we do now Dave?" Tariq asked, still trying to stop his teeth from chattering. Both of them were sitting on the trolley next to the Jones's empty car.

"Well, what we do now is we get on the Land Lord's plane, and get off at an appropriate point," Dave said in a matter of fact tone.

"How do we know what plane?" Tariq asked, a little more than just concerned.

"We know the plane because we can follow their luggage."

"How?" Tariq continued.

"Didn't you notice their luggage? It's not something you can miss very easily. All we need to do now is get to a position where we can see their luggage being loaded onto the plane and then jump on it."

"It's that simple?" Tariq asked.

"I hope so," said Dave.

Luckily for Dave and Tariq there was only one flight a day during the weekend, so working out which plane they had to get on was not really a problem.

Dave and Tariq made their way from the car to the fence that separated the car park from the airfield. After wandering up and down it a few times they found a small hole just about the right size to let them through, along with their trolley.

"Okay Dave, we're through the fence. What do we do now?"

"We wait," Dave replied.

"Wait for what?"

"We wait until we see the Land Lord's luggage of course."

"Okay. And then what?" said Tariq.

"And then we jump onto the luggage and by doing that, we get on the plane. Using the trolley we should be able to disguise ourselves as any other piece of luggage," Dave said, explaining his plan.

"Sometimes Dave I think you are a genius. This whole plan is brilliant."

"Actually Tariq this whole plan is crazy but it may just work," Dave said cautiously.

"And if it doesn't?" Tariq asked.

"If it doesn't then we have a holiday back at your place," Dave said, explaining the plan 'B' option.

"Oh," said Tariq.

The two friends waited and watched.

"There it is Tariq," Dave said pointing at the Jones's luggage. "Let's go for it."

They made their way as quickly as they could across the rough grass that separated them from the plane, but it was not fast enough. The airport staff were loading all the luggage in a very efficient and fast way, just as if they did this work every day of the week.

"I don't think we're going to make it," Dave said, disheartened.

"Neither do I," Tariq agreed. "Oh well, it was worth a try."

Dave was almost ready to give up on the idea, and then he remembered something Tariq had mentioned the day before. "Tariq, perhaps we still can. But this is totally dependent upon you."

"Why me?" Tariq asked.

"Because you know you can go a lot faster," Dave said.

"You mean you want me to ignore the faithful commitment that my kind made all those many years ago just to get us on a plane for a holiday?" Tariq said, realising what Dave was asking.

"Just this once Tariq. Please."

"I'm not sure that I can. Do you know what you're asking?"

"Yes, but I feel there is a good reason in this case," Dave said.

"You want me to break my kind's lore just for ourselves?" Tariq said, not happy with what he was being asked to do.

"No that wouldn't be right. *Just* for ourselves," Dave said. "I have a feeling we will be needed on Maiti."

"You're just making that up," said Tariq.

"Tariq, have you ever known me to make things up?" Dave said.

"No. You have a point there. Are you being truly honest?" Tariq said, still not totally sure about his friend's reasons.

"Yes. I am," Dave said, with the required commitment.

"Okay. Just this once. You know my ancestors will be shuddering in their graves don't you?"

"Just this once Tariq?" Dave implored.

"Okay Dave, just for you. Get in the trolley and hold tight," Tariq instructed.

Dave got in the trolley. They were still some 500 metres from the plane.

"You're not allowed to do this," Shell piped up.

"Shell, just shut up, this is important."

"Oh yeah?" Shell was not convinced.

"That is what I said last time and it was. This time is no different. Okay?" Tariq said to his shell quietly.

"No it's not Okay. How is going on holiday worth telling someone about the sacred pact and demonstrating the true potential of tortoise kind?" said Shell.

"I don't know Shell, but you will just have to trust me as I trust Dave."

"You're wrong, wrong, wrong, wrong, and when we get back be assured I will tell the elders." Shell threatened.

"Whatever," Tariq said.

"Who are you talking to Tariq?" Dave asked.

"No one. Just myself," Tariq said. Which was true in a way.

"Okay Tariq. You best do your best and get us to that plane."

Tariq stood up on his hind legs and lifted his shell as if he was pulling up a pair of baggy jeans that had somehow fallen around his ankles when he was about to go paddling.

"Give me the rope Dave." Tariq commanded. Dave handed him the rope.

All of a sudden Tariq's legs started moving, kicking up dust as their one, two, one two, motion increased. Around and around they went until they became just a blur. Then Tariq let loose. Dave nearly fell head over heels out of the back of the trolley as Tariq yanked it in the direction of the plane's loading bay. It was all he could do to hang on.

Within a blink of an eye Dave Tariq and the trolley, after a slight problem with stopping, were next to the container that now contained the Jones's luggage; a container which, very soon, was going to be loaded onto the plane.

"Blimey," said Dave. "If I wasn't a feather that had grown arms, legs and a nice yellow Lycra body suit, I wouldn't have believed it even if I'd tried."

"Dave there's no time for comment. We just need to get into that container," Tariq said abruptly. He was feeling a little guilty about using his incredible speed, something he shouldn't have done, but he dismissed his guilt and he and Dave got into the container. Tariq then passed Dave his shell suit and finally the trolley. After everything was loaded Tariq jumped in as well.

They sat in the cramped space uncertain what was going to happen next, though Dave thought he had some idea. Very soon there was a little jolt as the container was loaded onto the plane.

*

The first part of the plan had been a success. Dave and Tariq had got onto an aeroplane, one which was going to take them to the Caribbean, and this was all thanks to Tariq's secret ability. An ability that was not so secret anymore.

They sat in the cargo hold of flight MT309, which was already quite full, waiting for the other luggage to be loaded. Eventually the cargo bay door was slammed shut and both Tariq and Dave were plunged into darkness. Tariq wasn't happy. He'd never been in such a complete and alien darkness before, but he did have lights inside his shell for the purpose of cooking and reading of course.

"Dave?" Tariq asked quietly, unsure of what was going on. "Are we doing the right thing?"

"Tariq, don't worry," Dave chirped. "This is right, this is part of the plan," he continued in a reassuring way.

"You sure?" Tariq questioned again.

"Of course I'm sure. Just relax."

Tariq tried to relax in the completely dark place he now found himself in. He was sure Dave knew what he was doing but he wasn't 100 percent sure. Tariq resigned himself to the fact that there was not much else he could do about the situation anyway.

After about 30 minutes they felt the plane judder as it was shunted onto the taxiway, away from the stand. Once the plane was in the taxi lane, the pilot increased the speed of the engines. The plane was now ready to make its journey from England to the Caribbean.

"Dave we've done it. We are actually on our way. Tremendous." Tariq's mood was lifting a little.

A few moments after Tariq had spoken the plane accelerated down the runway and Dave, along with Tariq, was tumbled to the back of the container they were in.

"Whoaaa!" They both exclaimed.

"Dave what's happening?" Tariq asked once again, none too pleased with the way he had been thrown about the cargo hold.

"I believe we are taking off," Dave said calmly.

"Taking off! Taking off what? This doesn't feel like taking off anything. It feels like putting on," Tariq said, starting to get worried once more, as his weight seemed to increase at the same time as the roar of the plane's engines got louder.

"Taking off the ground," Dave said, realising Tariq had never flown before.

"I haven't got any ground on me Dave. What's happening?" Tariq was near to leaping out of his skin. Not that it would help at all.

"Tariq, just relax will you? The plane is off the ground and we are flying. Soon, I'm sure, the plane will level out and we can get back to feeling comfortable.

"Oh. Okay. Are you really sure?" Tariq implored.

"Of course I'm sure. I'm a feather aren't I?"

"Yes, I suppose you are," Tariq said, still not happy.

Chapter 12.
Five Sense and Some

After five hours of flight Tariq was getting jittery again. He was looking left and right, straining his eyes against the dark interior of the container they were in.

"Dave," Tariq started, "I've just had a worrying thought."

"What's that Tariq?"

"How do we know when we're there?"

"I'm sure there'll be a sign," said Dave. "And if not then we can rely on my seventh sense."

"Your seventh sense!"

"Yes. You know we all have five senses don't you?" Dave stated in his matter-of-fact manner.

"I do," Tariq agreed.

"And some living things have six," Dave continued.

"I have heard of the possibility."

"Well, feathers of my kind have a seventh sense," Dave explained. "All in all there is sight, sound, smell, taste, touch, which most things have. Then there is ESP, which is Extra Sensory Perception. And us feathers have TAP."

"TAP, what's that?" Tariq asked; he was curious.

"TAP, Tariq, is a sense of Time And Place. It's what allows us feathers to get our hosts, the migratory birds, the ones who feel the need to go south for the winter, or even north for the summer, from one place to another when they migrate. Without that they'd probably fly in circles for a long time and then settle back on their roosts believing they've actually gone somewhere, because they would feel exhausted!"

"Oh," Tariq said. "I wondered how they did that."

"Well now you know Tariq. The birds can get to where they go because of their feather's TAP ability."

Chapter 13.
The Announcement

The Jones's children were getting restless. They'd been on the plane for nearly nine hours.

"Are we nearly there yet?" said Maddy for the twentieth time that flight, fed up with being stuck in the cramped airline seats.

"Yeah, nearly there yet?" Jim piped up. "Where's my teddy?" he added.

"Calm down kids. Not much longer," their Dad replied.

Boing, boing, boing, went a noise.

"What's that noise Dad?" Maddy asked.

"I think the captain is going to make an announcement." Before John could say any more a voice came over the plane's intercom.

"Ladies and gentlemen we will be putting on the seat belt sign very shortly. We are currently flying at 10,000 feet and preparing to land. Can you please make your way back to your seats for the final approach? The cabin staff will come along to make sure your seats are upright, your trays folded and your seat belts are on. Just before we fly over the Caribbean island of Maiti you will feel a little jolt as we lower the undercarriage in preparation for landing at Montego Bay Airport, in Jamaica. I hope you have enjoyed your flight with AirCarib and look forward to seeing you for the return journey after your holidays."

"See, I told you we were nearly there Maddy. Sit back in your seat, put your tray up and put your seat belt on," her dad said.

"But it hurts, Daddy."

"Come on darling. Just do it. It's only a little while longer, before you can take your seat belt off again," her mother consoled.

Chapter 14.
10,000ft is Quite High Up

The captain's announcement had sounded out through the whole plane.

"Did you hear that Dave? It sounds like we're nearly there," Tariq said, excited for a change.

"That's what the captain said. I told you there would be a sign. We better get ready. Once the undercarriage goes down that's when we get off."

Tariq was so happy at the prospect of being on holiday. It never occurred to him what it meant to get off the plane before it had landed. The plane jolted and light began to seep into the cargo hold as the plane's landing gear was lowered.

"Right Tariq," Dave said suddenly. "We've got to get our stuff together. We're about to leave."

Dave and Tariq got their bits and pieces out of the container and made their way to the source of the light. As they got nearer the opening the wind picked up and Dave was nearly blown to the back of the cargo hold.

"Dave, I think it may be a good idea if you put your shell suit on. It's getting quite draughty."

"I think you're right Tariq. Good job you made sure I brought it with me." Dave put on his Concretonator shell suit. It was the suit Tariq had invented to help Dave get over his wind problem and it was certainly required now as he was suffering from the wind quite significantly. It would stop Dave from being blown about, as it was made from a special mixture of concrete and rubber.

"You know... I think we're quite high up and..." Tariq started, but before he could finish Dave had pushed Tariq out through the hole the plane's undercarriage had left when it had been lowered ready for landing. Dave jumped through the hole after him. The wind started to whistle past their ears as they fell towards the ground.

"Err..." Dave began.

"WHAT?" Tariq shouted through the air which was now whistling very loudly around them.

"I've just realised that I'm not really capable of flying in this suit. And worst of all..."

"And?" said Tariq, as they both travelled quite fast towards the ground.

Dave hesitated for a moment not knowing how to tell Tariq the whole problem in one sentence. He decided to forego any detail and said, "Neither are you."

*

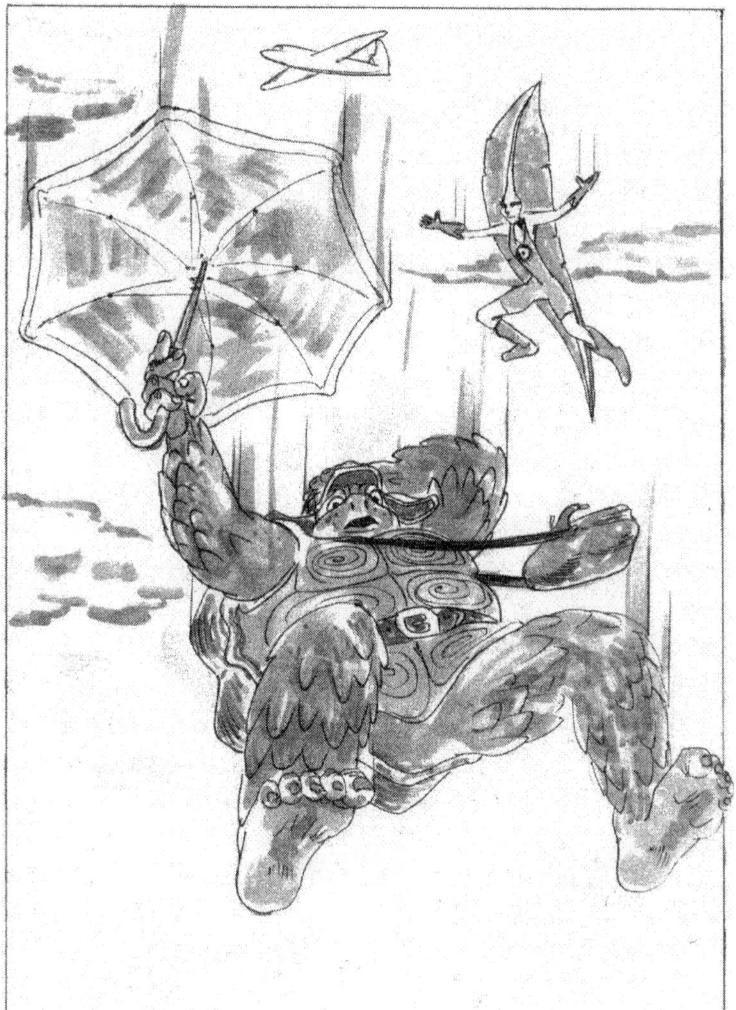

Tariq with his satchel, Dave in his shell suit and the trolley with their luggage were now hurtling to the ground, all attached together by a short piece of rope.

"What do you mean?" Tariq said, seriously concerned about this little bit of extra information.

"I just forgot. I'm so used to flying I didn't think about it."

"Oh my God," replied Tariq trying to get to grips with Dave's last statement.

"Oh well," said Dave. "I'm so sorry."

Tariq was astounded, so astounded he never considered what would happen when they reached the ground. How could it be that, he,

Tariq of the Insomniacs, actually Tariq the Gifted of the Insomniacs, had been brought all this way only to be pushed out of an aeroplane at 10,000 feet and all his friend could say was, 'I'm so sorry'?

Tariq was getting cross. So cross in fact that any thought about the inevitable crunch at the bottom, had left him. Oblivious to his impending doom Tariq reached into his satchel to get something, anything, anything at all he could use to bash Dave around the head, or any part of his stupid, feather shaped, yellow Lycra covered body for that matter, for getting him into this falling situation in the first place.

Tariq grabbed the first thing his hands happened upon in his satchel. It was his umbrella. And as he was about to make a swipe at Dave, the air caught the umbrella, opening it up. All of a sudden Tariq, Dave, the luggage and the trolley were descending in a much less hurried manner.

"That was such a brilliant idea Tariq," Dave exclaimed. "How did you think of that?"

"Well Dave, I knew I had to think of something," Tariq replied, not wanting Dave to know the real reason why he had reached into his satchel.

As they floated towards the ground, what had originally seemed to be an ordinary lumpy green field, gradually turned into the lush dark green tree tops of a jungle. They were about to land in one of the small patches of jungle which dotted the small Island of Maiti.

Chapter 15.
Mince Pies

"Dat was strange, Mon. D'you see dat mi old china?' said one of the island's inhabitants speaking in Caribbean Cockney Patois, to his friend. The man pointed to the bit of jungle that had just consumed Dave and Tariq as they disappeared through its canopy. Both the men were sitting on the porch of a small brightly coloured shack, taking in the mid-morning sun.

"See wot, Mon?" his friend said.

"See dat umbrella and de tortoise mon? Come from de sky mon?"

"Umbrella and de tortoise mon? Gwaan. Mi no Adam and Eve it Mon," his friend said, not believing a word.

"Yeh, Mon. Truss mi, mi no tell Pork Pies Mon," the man said trying to get across, to his friend, what he had just seen.

"Mon, you need de doctor, Mon, to fix dem Mince Pies, Mon," the friend said in a reassuring manner.

"Dey nutten wrong a fi mi Mince Pies, Mon," the man said giving up on the whole conversation.

They stopped talking and both men stared for a moment at the little bit of jungle from which a flock of birds had just flown into the air, and then they looked at their beer cans. Eyeing each other quickly they shook their heads and in unison they began to rock back and forth in their chairs once again, supping their beer, wondering what had or had not been seen.

Chapter 16.
Landing and TAP

Dave and Tariq crashed slowly through the jungle's green canopy.

"Ooph."

CRACK,

"Ow."

CRUNCH

"Arh."

BOOMPH

They landed on the soft loamy soil of the jungle floor.

"That wasn't too bad," said Dave as he stood up and brushed himself off.

"Not too bad Dave. But please tell me next time you expect me to leap out of a plane which was, at my guess, at least 10,000 feet from the ground."

"Yeah. Sorry about that. I think I got a little bit carried away. Haven't flown for a long time you know," Dave said, attempting to explain his actions.

"Flown? You call that flying? You fell like a feather covered in concrete."

"Okay Tariq. I'll make sure I have a better plan next time."

"You think there's going to be a next time then?" Tariq said.

"Err… well… probably not. But just in case I'll have a better plan anyway," Dave said.

"What do we do now, Mr Genius?" Tariq said sarcastically. He was still cross at what he had been put through.

"Tariq. We're here now. Safe and sound."

"I know. I'm sure I'll relax soon," Tariq said, acknowledging his terse response.

"Follow me. I'll get us to our holiday spot and then we can enjoy the rest of the time we have here."

"How do you know where you're going?"

"TAP," responded Dave, tapping his forehead.

"TAP? Oh yeah," Tariq said remembering. "Time And Place."

"Correct," said Dave. "You ready?"

"I think so," said Tariq.

"Just let me take this shell suit off. Then we'll go."

Dave got out of his Concretonator suit, dumped it in the trolley, and then strode off in the direction of the deep jungle, pulling the trolley behind him. Tariq followed.

After a few hundred metres it seemed it was going to be impossible to go any further. The jungle was closing in; all the bushes, leaves and creepers around them were getting thicker.

"Dave, are you sure this is the right way?" Tariq asked.

"TAP, Tariq, TAP. Just remember that," Dave replied.

"Okay, TAP, TAP, I'll remember it. But what are you going to do about all these plants?" Tariq asked.

"Well, a thought did occur to me, and I was just wondering whether you may have brought something with you that could help us out."

"Help us out in what? — You know what you're doing. Don't you?" Tariq was concerned.

"Help us out in this situation," Dave said.

"Situation?" said Tariq, even more concerned. This was the first time he had been told he was in a, '*situation*'.

"Yes," Dave continued. "It seems the path is blocked."

"I'll have a look, but nothing springs to mind," Tariq said, proceeding to look through his satchel. There were no knives, no machetes, actually no blades of any kind and nothing at all to cut a path through the jungle, not even a flat piece of shiny metal.

"Dave, I think we're a bit stuck. I don't seem to have anything. Sorry."

"What's that?" Dave said, pointing to what looked like the end of a slim lampshade that was now sticking out of Tariq's satchel.

"Oh that. It's nothing really. Probably the most *stupidest* invention I have ever created," Tariq said, quietly hoping Dave hadn't heard him admit to creating something stupid.

"What is it Tariq?"

Tariq looked shame faced. "It's a torch that shines nothing," he said, highly embarrassed.

"A light that shines nothing," Dave thought out loud. "A torch that, possibly, shines dark light. You are a wonder Tariq."

"I know; it's truly stupid," Tariq admitted.

"No Tariq, not by any means. Does it work?"

"Well, it's got its own power, and it doesn't shine, apart from that I don't know how to tell whether it works or not."

"Give it here," Dave requested, holding out his hand. Tariq passed the lampshade-shaped torch, which shined nothing, over to Dave.

"Let me show you Tariq," Dave said. Not having the slightest idea of how this duff invention was going to help them out but he took hold of it anyway.

Dave was getting more and more confident in Tariq's crackpot inventions, however barmy they seemed to be. He knew they could sometimes backfire, but on the whole, they seemed to pan out, eventually.

Dave turned on the dark light and pointed it ahead.

"See. Nothing," Tariq said. "I don't know why you even considered it."

"Just wait a minute Tariq," Dave said, wishing his friend would have some patience.

Dave was pointing the dark light directly ahead at the dense vegetation. Slowly the vegetation and its leaves gradually rolled back revealing a path ahead.

"See?"

"What's happening?" Tariq asked.

"I think your dark light is persuading the bushes that it's really night-time, and everybody knows that, at night, plants and certain other vegetation curl up when there is no light. Once the plants have finished believing it's not daytime any longer, we will then be able to proceed."

Slowly but surely the plants in Dave's and Tariq's path gradually pulled back leaving them with a track to follow.

"That's tremendous," said Tariq.

"Only due to your invention," Dave conceded.

Dave and Tariq made their way through the rest of the jungle quite easily. It was only when they came across a fence that they had to stop.

"A fence Dave," said Tariq, stating the obvious.

"I know. But do you know what?"

"No Dave, I don't," Tariq said.

"This is where we'll have our holiday."

"By a fence?" said Tariq feeling more miserable than he had done so far, when it seemed they would not be able to make their way through the jungle.

"No, on the other side of the fence. This is our holiday resort," Dave stated confidently.

Chapter 17.
Gilbert Bates

It was mid-morning at the Royal DeMacaroon Club Carib resort and Gilbert Bates, plus entourage, namely his Personal Assistant, Gene Baubs, who he took everywhere with him, entered the breakfast bar.

"Gilbert. What are you going to have for brunch?" Gene asked.

Gilbert Bates, a short, balding, bespectacled and very successful business man, stared sternly at his number two. "How many times do

I have to tell you not to call me Gilbert, I am Gil. Okay?"

"Sorry, sir," said, Gene Baubs.

"Okay, Gene, not a problem. You *will* remember now won't you?" Gil said reinforcing his statement.

"Okay," Gene replied.

"You won't forget?"

"No, sir. I won't forget," Gene replied, attempting to reinforce his loyalty.

"That's good, Gene. Neither will I," Gil stated, trying to be sure that he had got across his view on failure.

"Oh!" said, Gene, not being able to think of anything else to say.

"What's on the menu then?" Gil asked.

"Er, there's bacon, sausage, bread, tomato, egg, sausage and bread," Gene Baubs replied.

"Ah. I like the sound of sausage. Is there any food that starts with Mike? Because I like food that starts with Mike, and I'm on holiday, and I don't want to be upset."

Gilbert Bates's PA blinked at the request, he was used to all sorts of strange requests from his boss but he was struggling now. He definitely didn't want to upset his boss any further, especially as he was on holiday.

An idea sprung into, Gene Baubs's head. "There's mike-cro-waved mushroom, sir," he said.

"That sounds good, Gene. I'll have some of that as well."

Gene left his boss at the breakfast table and went to the breakfast bar to order the bacon, sausage, tomato, bread, egg and sausage brunch, plus a side helping of mushrooms, which he asked to be microwaved.

Gil sat at the breakfast table and looked around, then sighed almost happily.

What a brilliant place to be, he thought. He also started thinking about how he could make some more money.

Gene came back with his breakfast platter. "Here you are, sir."

"Well thank you very much, Gene."

"A pleasure, sir, as always."

Gilbert Bates finished his breakfast.

"Gene?"

"Yes, sir," he replied.

"I want to make more money," Gil said matter-of-factly.

"Naturally, sir."

"How should I go about this?" Gil questioned his PA.

"I'm not sure, sir."

"NOT SURE?" Gil yelled. "What do I pay you for? I certainly don't pay you to sit around thinking of nothing."

"No, that's true, sir. I just wasn't ready for the question," Gene said attempting, but failing, to get out of the predicament he had been put into.

Chapter 18.
Holiday Home

Whilst Gil was questioning his PA, Dave and Tariq were scrambling over the fence into the resort.

"Dave, once we're over the fence, where are we going to stay?"

"It's obvious Tariq," Dave said. "We'll need to find a place where we can rest without any interruption for the next two weeks."

"I know that, but where is it?"

Dave looked around at the resort and tapping in to his TAP ability he pointed towards an outhouse that looked like it hadn't been used for a long time.

"Over there?" Tariq asked.

"No," said Dave.

"No?"

"Yes. No," said Dave again.

"Okay Dave, then where?"

"Over there." Dave pointed again to the chalet behind the outhouse; on its door hung a sign saying that it was closed for refurbishment.

"In there?" Tariq said.

"Naturally," said Dave. "It's a little room that is in need of some paint and other stuff which certainly won't be fixed until the end of the holiday season. We'll be perfectly safe in there." With that statement made, they sneaked through the resort to the closed chalet.

"Right, let's go in," said Dave and shoved the door. The door wouldn't budge. "Erm, Tariq, I think I could do with some help here." They both pushed the door and it opened, slowly revealing a dark interior.

They entered and closed the door behind them discovering why the door had been so hard to open. The chalet was being used as a storeroom, of sorts, and part of an unstable pile of holiday resort bits had collapsed and wedged against the door.

"I don't think this place is as unused as you thought it was Dave."

"Believe me Tariq, this place won't be disturbed until the refurbishment. Everything in here is here for a reason."

Tariq still wasn't sure. "What reason?"

"It's here so that it's ready to be used when they decide to redecorate and paint this place."

Tariq and Dave looked around; there were pots of paint, curtain material, paint brushes and hammers, in fact everything that was needed to fix up a broken down chalet.

"This is our room for our holiday," Dave said, pleased.

Chapter 19.
My Little Rat

"Gene," Gil said firmly. "I haven't brought you here for a holiday."

"Yes sir, I understand, sir."

"I'm here for a rest," his boss continued, "and you're here to help me. Okay?"

"Yes, sir, absolutely right sir."

"So how are you going to help me think of something that can make me lots of money?" Gil asked.

"I'm not quite sure sir," said, Gene foolishly.

"Gene, what do I pay you for? I don't pay you not to think, do I, Gene?" Gilbert Bates said.

"Yes sir, I mean no sir, I mean of course, sir. Absolutely correct sir."

"WELL?" Gil demanded. "What's your idea?"

"Err. What about..." Gene was struggling to think of something. He wasn't good under pressure.

"Come on, Gene, tell me."

"Err...," Gene Baubs said again.

"Err, is not good enough. TELL ME SOMETHING," Gil shouted.

"How about an egg fountain? Everyone eats eggs."

"And how exactly will that work, Gene?" Gil asked, more than slightly annoyed.

"Well... there's a fountain... and there's some eggs... and the eggs go into the fountain... and then you have an egg fountain," Gene said, wishing he hadn't.

"Gene, I think that is the most stupid idea I have ever heard. You have to do better," his boss demanded.

Gene looked out of the breakfast bar attempting to get some inspiration, an idea, something that would please his boss. He saw the children in the swimming pool, he saw their parents smiling at them and he saw a child crying. He sighed inwardly. Poor kid he thought.

Then he saw the kid's dad take a cuddly bear to the child and the child stopped crying. An idea sprung into his head.

"Gilbert, what about..." Before he could finish Gilbert Bates exploded.

"GENE! How many times have I told you not to call me Gilbert? What DO I pay you for?"

"Very sorry sir. I meant to say, cuddly toys."

Gilbert Bates thought about this for a moment, and after a very long pause he said, "Gene, I think you have something there. What a good idea; soft toys. I'm sure I can do something with this. I mean, there are so many children in the world, an untapped resource in fact. Especially if the only toy they want is one of mine."

"Sir, I believe you've hit the nail on the proverbial head."

"I believe I have, Gene. I believe I have," Gil said, very happy with his idea. "Where do we go from here?"

"Well," Gene said. "Christmas is coming up very fast. Perhaps we could get your cuddly toys into the shops for that."

"Sometimes, Gene, you surprise me. I think I'll have to get my cuddly toys out in the shops before Christmas."

"What a good idea sir. I doubt that anyone would have thought of that," Gene said, feeling relieved.

"Gene, we need a catchy name for them, something that everyone will remember and want. A name that will be on everyone's lips, something they will always think of when they think of toys."

"Absolutely, sir. How about..." Gene racked his brains for a catchy name. "How about... Comfort Boys?" He said after digging deep into the memory of his younger days.

"No, I don't think that would do it. It sort of skips 50 percent of the market," Gil said, then added, "You don't have a girlfriend do you, Gene?"

"Of course not sir," Gene replied. "My loyalties are with you and your company. sir."

"That's good to hear, Gene — I think. Any better names spring to mind?"

"What about Furry Tots?"

"No. That sounds like kids with beards. I don't think that would work."

"My Little Rat?" Gene carried on.

"Possibly, but I don't think the parents would go for it."

"Squeezy Freds?" Gene said hopefully.

"No, Gene, it just doesn't have the ring to it. I think you're going in the right direction though. Scrap the 'Fred' bit."

"Softy Mikes?"

"Softy Mikes," Gil mulled over the idea. "I think you have it."

"Softy Mikes?" Gene questioned. He was extremely surprised at his boss's acceptance of the idea.

"Yes, Gene, my fine PA," Gil said. "My next venture, what I will do next, is create the cuddly toys …," Gil went on, his voice rising, "called — Softy Mikes." A *ta-da* noise chimed silently in, Gene's head, and his boss continued. "These toys will be everything the kids want. In fact, they will not want anything else." Gilbert Bates finished; a small and evil grin creeping across his face as he uttered the last few words. He rubbed his hands together.

Chapter 20.
Perception is Nine Tenths of the Look

After unloading their holiday gear in the chalet, Dave and Tariq decided they ought to join in with all the activities the resort offered.

There was only one problem though; they were a tortoise and a feather and probably couldn't mingle with the rest of the holidaymakers easily without some disguise. All of a sudden an idea popped into Tariq's head.

"I think we need a disguise."

"I think you're right Tariq," Dave agreed.

"What we need to do is look like everyone else, in such a way that we'll be noticed as much as the other guests are."

"Good idea, but how are we going to do that?" Dave said. Tariq looked around the inside of the chalet.

"Perhaps," Tariq said thinking aloud, "we don't look like holidaymakers."

"Sorry Tariq, not quite with you. Are you suggesting we ought to look like us?"

"No. Of course not," Tariq retorted. "Perhaps we could look like the staff or the entertainers here or even the locals. There's certainly enough stuff in here to do that."

"What are you suggesting Tariq?"

*

"Well, you see those curtains over there?" Tariq said.

"Yeah," said Dave, beginning to get worried about what was going to be suggested next.

"I'm sure we could turn those into something that looks like local dress."

"You want me to go out in a dress made of curtain?"

"No. Not just you, we both go out there. We make a dress and you stand on my shoulders. The dress would cover us."

"Tariq," said Dave, "I don't like the way you're thinking, but I think we'll have to give it a go anyway."

Tariq walked around the room, picking up bits of material, rolls of sequins, and bits of carpet underlay, and then got to work. Within the hour he had created a dress that looked almost exactly like the dresses they had seen the local women wearing. The only difference, in this case, was that the dress stood up of its own accord without anyone being in it.

"Tariq, sometimes you astound me."

"I know. It's good isn't it?" Tariq said, proud with his creation.

"No, it's not good. And you won't catch me in that ever."

"Oh!" Tariq said, dismayed by his friend's reaction.

"Tariq, I'm going to suggest something that doesn't appear all that obvious in the first place, but it's quite likely to work."

"What's that?"

"We go out as we are," said Dave.

"AS WE ARE?" Tariq replied utterly astounded.

"Yes, as we are... well almost, anyway," Dave said.

"How are we going to make that work?" Tariq said, confused about the whole idea.

"All we need to do is leave this chalet, with the appropriate flip-flops and sunglasses on, in such a way that it can only be assumed we're tourists, and we won't be noticed."

"Flip-flops and sunglasses?" Tariq repeated.

"Perception is nine tenths of the look," Dave said in a wise manner.

"Nine tenths?"

"Yep. Nine tenths," Dave confirmed.

"Okay Dave. But if anyone tries to put me in a race against a hare, I will not be pleased. I get enough of that back home."

"So we're agreed then?" Dave said.

"We are, as you put it, agreed." With the conversation finished Dave put on his sunglasses and Tariq, after a little searching around, found some flip-flops for them both.

"I've no sunglasses," Tariq said ignoring a pair sitting on the chalet shelf.

"Tariq there's a pair right there," said Dave, pointing at a pair of glasses that consisted of two lenses, obviously, and each lens was surrounded by many small and pink plastic clam shells, in a variety of shades.

"No Dave, not them," Tariq implored.

Dave looked at Tariq sternly. "Tariq, you'll be surprised how well they will work and don't forget you suggested a dress. No one will ever have a clue that you're a tortoise."

"Why?" said Tariq, not convinced.

"Because tortoises don't wear pink clam shell sunglasses."

After a few moments thought, and with no way to counter Dave's argument, Tariq took the clam shell sunglasses from the shelf opposite, and put them on; not at all pleased.

"You look great," Dave said and pulled open the door to their chalet, smiling a little to himself. They were ready to holiday.

*

It was a bright and sunny morning. There were a few small, white fluffy clouds dotting the incredibly blue sky, and the holiday resort guests were making their way back to their own chalets and apartments, having finished their brunch. They were going to get ready for the rest of the day's lounging around in the Caribbean sun on the small island of Maiti.

"Now remember Tariq, act like a tourist," Dave said, shutting the door to their chalet behind them.

Dave and Tariq made their way into the resort proper, leaving the chalet area, looking forward to what they would find on offer.

Chapter 21.
Pedalo Power

After letting his breakfast go down Gilbert Bates wondered what he could do next as part of his holiday experience. He wasn't very good at holidays because, wherever he was, all he could ever think about was money and making huge piles of it at that.

His dream was to make enough money so he could use his left over coins, and notes, to make bricks and window frames out of them, for his next house. Then when the house was finished he would have a car built out of his remaining spare cash, but using only the notes this time. He smiled to himself at these thoughts and rubbed his hands together as he always did, when he thought about money. Then he remembered what his overpaid therapist had told him.

'Mr Bates, if you carry on thinking only of your work you will make yourself ill. It's about time you had a holiday'. Though he hadn't liked what he had been told, he hated the idea of being ill even more, because if he got ill he wouldn't be able to make any more money, and that thought alone made him feel sick. So he had gone on holiday, as suggested, to the

Caribbean island of Maiti taking only his PA, Gene Baubs, with him.

Gilbert Bates looked around. What could he do next now he was on holiday? He glanced out of the resort over the golden sands of its beach, at the crystal clear Caribbean Sea, and listened to the shushing of the small waves as they lapped against the shore.

I will go sailing in a pedalo, he thought to himself. "GENE," he called at the top of his voice just because he could. "I want to go sailing in a pedalo. Arrange it for me."

"Of course, sir," Gene said and got up from the breakfast table to arrange his boss's entertainment. Gene walked over to the Water Sports kiosk.

"Excuse me," Gene said to the man at the kiosk who was sitting with his feet up on the desk, listening to the local music on the radio.

"Yeah, Mon?" the man replied.

"Pardon me?" Gene said, realising this holiday was going to take some getting used to.

The man in the kiosk rolled his eyes; then putting on his best American accent he said, "Yes, sir. How may I help you?" Moving his head slightly from side to side with each word he uttered.

Within half an hour, Gene Baubs and Gilbert Bates were getting into a bright yellow pedalo;

Gilbert Bates sat in the front and, Gene sat behind him on the seat that had the peddles to make the boat go.

"Well done, Gene," Gil said as the man from the kiosk pushed them from the resort's jetty. "Where are you going to take me sailing then?" he asked as he put his feet up over the front of the pedalo.

"I don…," before, Gene finished his sentence he decided it probably wasn't the best thing to say and finished, "You see that small yellowy island over there."

"Yes, Gene."

"I think we'll go there. I've got a picnic together." Gene pointed at the hamper he had brought with him and then at the small, apparently sandy, island in the distance; an island whose yellowness was just visible on the horizon.

"Don't you think that's a bit too far, Gene?"

"No, sir. Of course not, sir. It's just the way the air here makes it look."

"Are you sure?" Gil asked, after he had removed, cleaned and replaced his round lensed spectacles to see if it would make the island look any closer, but it didn't.

"Absolutely, sir," Gene said as he bit the knuckles of his clenched fist, truly wishing he hadn't said that.

"Well then. Off we go," his boss said. "What a good idea."

Gene shuddered. His boss now thought this was a good idea and even before they began to make their way to the island, Gene was already regretting it.

After an hour on the calm and crystal sea the island still seemed to be the same distance away. Even the resort's beach now seemed to be the same size as the island, Gene had suggested they ought to go to.

Gene peddled on and as the sun started its way back towards the horizon the pedalo landed on the small island's beach.

"Well done, Gene," his boss said, seemingly very happy. "I'm quite hungry now but the journey was worth it." Gil got off the pedalo and made his way up the beach and sat down. Perhaps his therapist wasn't paid too much after all.

"Gene, come on," Gil called to his PA.

"I can't," Gene said.

Gil started frowning. "What do you mean you can't? What do I …"

"I don't think my legs are working," Gene said quickly, hoping to calm his boss's obvious anger, but it was to no avail.

"What do you mean your legs aren't working? You've been sitting down for the last few hours, as I have, and my legs are working fine."

"Be with you in a minute, sir," Gene called from the pedalo, and then proceeded to grab each of his legs in turn, very slowly lifting each of them over the side of the boat.

Both his numb legs were now dangling in the shallow, crystal clear water and after a few moments wondering whether he should do anything else, and with a quick glance at his boss, Gene decided it would be best if he joined his boss further up the island's beach. He lifted himself onto the side of the pedalo and then dropped into the water, promptly slipping beneath the sea's surface as his legs gave way when he tried to stand on the seabed.

"GENE," Gil yelled. "Can you bring the food?" Gilbert Bates's voice penetrated the water as if it was nothing but air.

"Bleb, Blur," Gene replied, making his first ever effort at answering his boss's questions from the wrong side of the sea's surface. Within a few moments, Gene had used his arms to pull himself up above the water and onto the beach.

"What was that, Gene?" Gilbert Bates asked.

"Yes, sir," Gene replied again, now that he was no longer under the water.

"Good man," Gil said. "Can I have the salmon sandwiches? You *have* brought salmon sandwiches haven't you?"

Fortunately for, Gene he had.

"Here you are, sir," Gene said, staggering up the beach in a zigzag fashion; after convincing his legs that they really ought to start working again.

Gilbert Bates took the sandwiches and scoffed them down just as, Gene was about to make himself comfortable on the soft sand of the beautiful island he'd paddled them to.

After finishing the last salmon sandwich Gil wiped his mouth with a napkin as he looked at the sun. "I think it's time we ought to be getting back," he said. "I don't want to miss the evening's entertainment."

"No, sir. You don't," Gene replied, gritting his teeth. Sometimes his boss could be a little demanding.

"Okay. We better get back then, Gene. Off to the boat." Gil got up from the beach and began to make his way back to the yellow pedalo.

Whilst still sitting, Gene packed up their picnic. He slung the hamper over his shoulder and after a few moments of failing to stand he decided against walking at all. Letting himself fall onto his stomach, he used his arms and hands in a front crawl fashion to drag the picnic basket down the beach towards the pedalo and the waiting Gilbert Bates; his legs still hadn't recovered from the journey out to the island.

"I've never seen that before, Gene."

"What's that, sir?"

"The way you made your way down the beach. Is this what one does on holiday?"

"Yes, sir," Gene replied, lying. "I'm just getting into the holiday zone. That's all."

"I think," Gil said, "I'll have to try that while we're here. It seems like it could be fun."

Gene didn't say anything and loaded up the pedalo, gingerly getting back into his seat ready to paddle his boss back to the resort.

"Well, Gene," Gil said. "We can't miss the start of this evening's entertainment. Best we get a move on."

"Yes, sir," Gene said, making a mental note to be more careful about the suggestions he made during the next ten days.

By the time Gil and, Gene had arrived back at the resort's jetty, dusk had settled and the night's entertainment was soon about to start.

Chapter 22.
Wrapping Entertainment

"Dave," Tariq exclaimed, removing his pink clam shell glasses as they made their way back to the chalet Dave had found for their holiday. "This place is tremendous. I've never been on holiday before. This is so good."

"I knew you would like it, Tariq."

"The beach, the restaurant, the fruit juices; I've never been anywhere like this; it is so good." Tariq said again. He was getting into the holiday mood.

"Apart from all that, are you okay with your sunglasses?"

"I think I can put up with them — now," Tariq said. He had got used to the idea, especially as it had worked.

"What do you want to do next?" Dave asked, pleased that Tariq had got over his drop of 10,000 feet just to get here.

"I like the idea of seeing the person who's advertised on one of the notice boards."

"Which person?"

"DJ Wrapper of course. I think it's going to be a great show, judging by the poster. It starts at 7.00pm."

"Well Tariq. That's what we'll do then. We'll go and listen to DJ Wrapper's set, when it's on. We've got a little while to wait yet though."

"Tremendous!"

Dave and Tariq moved the only two chairs they had in their chalet outside, so they could sit down in the warm early evening and take in the sea views, listen to the noises of animals they didn't even know the names of, and drink the Caribbean fruit juices they had brought back from the free drinks bar, next to the swimming pool.

This is the life, Dave thought to himself.

Chapter 23.
A Pay Rise!

Gilbert Bates walked back to his room with, Gene hobbling behind.

"Gene, I don't know why you took so long to get us back," Gil moaned at his PA. "I mean; it didn't take you that long to get us there in the first place. What is wrong with you?"

"Well, sir," Gene started his careful reply. "I believe it was something to do with the tidal currents and the wind." He was trying to give a reasonable explanation without letting on as to why it had taken him so long to get back. He couldn't let his boss know, ever, that his legs had never been up to the journey in the first place., Gene thought that if he had mentioned this, then Gil might start thinking he wasn't up to the job of being a Personal Assistant for him either. He needed his job as it was the only thing he knew how to do.

"Anyway," Gil said, "you got us back, albeit late, but you did get us back. It is for this reason and this reason alone, I will pay for the night's entertainment and you won't have to — as long as you are ready when I am."

"Thank you, sir," Gene said, not too happy and wobbling a lot.

"Gene, I think I am liking this holiday idea. It's a break for me."

"So am I, sir," Gene replied, not meaning it at all.

"I'm enjoying it so much I think I'm going to have to give you a pay rise."

Gene was stunned for a long moment, hearing this from his boss. But as soon as he had regained his senses he said, "So am I, sir. I couldn't think of any better holiday." He had changed his mind about how he had felt a few moments before.

"I knew you would think that, Gene, that's why I brought you here. After we've prepared ourselves, what do you think we should do next on this holiday of ours?"

"I think," Gene said, recalling the posters he'd noticed plastered across the resort's walls, whilst he'd been arranging his boss's pedalo trip, "we ought to see this DJ Wrapper. He sounds like he's going to be quite good."

"Well, if that's so, then you ought to be getting me ready, Gene."

"Of course, sir."

As soon as, Gene had finished preparing his boss for the evening's entertainment he got himself ready. He put on a light-weight checked jacket and denim jeans. Beneath the jacket he wore a light pink shirt with a largish collar, which he'd unbuttoned to the top of his chest showing off glimpses of his golden chain. On the jacket's lapel he'd pinned a small coral coloured flower. Then finally, after checking to make sure his boss wasn't looking, he adjusted his black toupee. It was the only secret he kept from his boss. They were now ready to sit in the restaurant, which looked out on the resort's entertainments area, to watch the show.

Gene left their ground floor apartment and found a suitable table in the entertainment area, which was just outside the restaurant where they'd eaten their breakfast earlier that day. Then he went back to the holiday apartment, collecting his boss, and shortly after that, they were both seated waiting for the evening's show to begin.

Chapter 24.
Displays and Swizzle Sticks

It was dark now and the night was still pleasantly warm. Dave and Tariq were looking for a place to sit, somewhere where they wouldn't be noticed even though they had their sunglasses and flip-flops to disguise them.

It didn't take long to find the right place; it was close to the stage, somewhere the resort's other guests had decided not to sit, possibly because of the expected volume of the DJ's show.

Their table was just off to the right of the venue's stage and out of the glare of its spotlights. It was perfect.

Dave and Tariq made themselves comfortable in the dimly lit area, looking forward to the evening and the show they were about to see.

"Isn't this just tremendous Dave? We're here, on holiday, watching a show. Tremendous!"

"Tariq, this is what a holiday is about; relaxing and enjoying."

"Yeah." Was all Tariq could say before the thrumming music started to play, indicating the beginning of the show.

The lights began to pulse in time with the Reggae music; the bass beats rattling the audience's ribcages and rattling a few of the guest's badly placed wine glasses onto the floor at the same time. Monkey-like creatures climbed on top of the restaurant's roof ready to listen to the music they had come to enjoy, and learn. The music, or at least the notes, were something they would sing to one another when the moon was out. They kept to the shadows so they wouldn't be disturbed while they wrote down the tunes on old palm fronds.

Fireworks at the front of the stage exploded in red, gold and green; the small island's national colours. After they had died away dancers sprang onto the stage from either side; shimmying their dresses in time to the beat of the music.

The darkness of the night was now complete and the continuing lightshow used this to its advantage. Red, gold and green lights flashed on and off. Red, gold and green fireworks zipped into the air with a *ffffzzzzzzit*, sound, then exploded with a booming bass *SCHTUMA!* thrum. And still the dancers flowed from the left of the stage, and from the right of the stage, moving in unison with the music, the lights and the fireworks. Coloured smoke drifted lazily across the wooden platform of the performance area from the spent pyrotechnics and the audience was in awe; they sat completely silent, mouths agape, enthralled, watching the display.

*

After the dancers had finished their piece, the music died away and the stagehands started to change the set ready for DJ Wrapper's spot.

*

"Dave," Tariq said, now that he was able to be heard, "would you like another glass of juice with an umbrella in it?"

"That's a good idea Tariq. Perhaps you could see if they do swizzle sticks as well," Dave said. He was also getting into the holiday mood.

Tariq left the table and made his way to the bar. *Umbrellas and swizzle sticks*, Tariq thought. His friend was certainly beginning to enjoy himself.

*

"Gene," Gilbert Bates said, attracting his PA's attention.

"Yes Gilbert," Gene replied, not thinking about what he was saying.

"Do I have to tell you……"

"No, sir. Sorry, sir," Gene said; his attention now fully focused on his boss. "What I meant to say was, yes, sir."

"I'll let that little mistake go," Gilbert Bates conceded. "What I was trying to say was; we need to start planning …." Before he was able to finish he noticed the person who was meant to be DJ Wrapper, walking from his dressing room towards the stage. "Gene…… have a look at that man over there." Gil pointed. "Does he remind you of anyone?"

Gene looked. "Do you mean the man in the red velvet t-shirt with white furry trimmings and the red velvet shorts?"

"Yes. That's exactly the man I was meaning," Gil said.

"The man with the floppy red hat and big bushy white beard, with small gold rimmed spectacles and red velvet flip-flops with white fluffy pom-poms on?"

"Yes, Gene: *that* man. I seem to have vague memories of him. Do you know who he is?" Gil said slowly, as he tried to recollect where he had seen him before.

"If I'm not mistaken," Gene began to respond, very cautiously, "it could almost be Santa Claus, if he wasn't DJ Wrapper of course."

Gilbert Bates hit the table very hard, their drinks jumping a few centimetres into the air. "Gene," Gil began firmly. Gene cringed, not wanting his boss to go on, but his boss did anyway. "Gene, I believe you're right. Go and find out."

Although relieved by his boss's response, Gene didn't have any idea how to find out, without 'Santa Claus' disguising who he really was if, in fact, he was *the* Santa Claus.

As if reading his PA's mind Gil said, "What you need to do is ask for his autograph and just before he is about to sign it, distract his attention. That way you may be able to get him to sign his real name."

"Okay," Gene replied, appreciating his boss's cunning.

Gene crossed the floor of the open air concert area and wandered up to the man in red velvet who was now standing at the side of the stage waiting for his equipment to be set up.

"Er," Gene said, stopping in front of the man in red. The man turned to face him.

"Yo ho," the man said. "What can I do for you?"

"Could I have your autograph please?"

"Ho, ho, ho. Of course you can sonny. Have you a pen and paper?"

"Yes Ssss...., sir, here," Gene stammered as he shakily handed DJ Wrapper a pen and a piece of paper. He was a little bit in awe of the superstar of the Royal DeMacaroon Club Carib resort, and was worried that DJ Wrapper might see through the whole plan.

Just as DJ Wrapper was about to sign the paper, Gene piped up, "Have you seen that strange looking roof tile over there?" He pointed to the palm-frond covered roof of the restaurant complex.

DJ Wrapper looked at where, Gene was pointing and frowned, he couldn't see any roof tiles. He continued to scribble his signature onto the paper, wondering what on earth the person was going on about. Before the man in red could think of anything else, Gene said, "I appreciate your work."

"Ho, ho, ho. Why thank you son," DJ Wrapper said, handing the piece of paper and pen back and patting him on the head.

Gene returned quickly to his boss's table before the DJ could say or do anything else. He placed the piece of paper on the table. Gil picked it up, and looking at it, he smiled.

"Well, well, well," Gil said, still smiling. "What a turn up for the books."

"What?" Gene asked.

Gilbert Bates showed, Gene the signature.

"It says Santa Claus," Gene said. "Why did DJ Wrapper sign himself as Santa Claus?"

"Roast me some sushi, Gene!" Gil said, very surprised at his PA's response. "You really don't know?"

"Sir. You're not telling me that DJ Wrapper is really Santa Claus — are you?"

"Of course I'm telling you that. And you know what this means don't you?" Gil said smiling his evil smile.

"No," Gene replied.

Gilbert Bates began to explain his dastardly plan.

*

At the same moment Gilbert Bates was explaining to, Gene his next course of action to make sure his Softy Mike cuddly toys idea worked, Tariq was wandering past the end of their table on his way to the bar to collect more fruit juices for Dave and himself.

Tariq paused momentarily as the conversation on the table next to him wafted into his ears. He could not believe what he was hearing. He slowed down his stride, which was a bit difficult as he couldn't go much slower being a tortoise in flip-flops, so he could hear a little more but before Tariq could hear the rest of what was being said DJ Wrapper put on the signature tune that meant his set was beginning.

Tariq, knowing it would be pointless to try and listen further, made his way to the bar and collected two more glasses of fruit juice, making sure Dave's one had an umbrella and a swizzle stick in it. As quickly as he could, he made his way back to his and Dave's table, very excited, but just a little bit worried as well.

Chapter 25.
The Evil Doers' Dastardly Plan

"Dave, you won't believe what I've just heard," Tariq said as he placed their glasses of fruit juice on the table.

"What?" Dave asked, curious as to why his friend seemed so agitated.

"I think Santa Claus is here and……"

Before Tariq could finish Dave interrupted. "Santa Claus! — Is here on Maiti?"

"Yes," Tariq said, "but not only that, there are two people here who want to change all of his presents to cuddly toys."

"Is that a bad thing Tariq? Surely there's nothing wrong with cuddly toys?"

"But they're planning to make sure there is only one cuddly toy for all the children at Christmas."

"Just one?" Dave said, now understanding why Tariq had seemed so agitated.

"Yes," Tariq replied. "Only one and it will be called a Softy Mike."

"That's not good," Dave said, a bad feeling coming over him, forcing his holiday mood to disappear and knowing it had now been banished for the rest of the trip.

"No it's not," Tariq agreed, imagining how Jim and Maddy Jones would feel about their Christmas if this happened.

"How are they going to do that?"

"I don't know. The music started before I could hear the rest," Tariq sighed.

"How on earth are they going to make sure that Santa Claus only gives out the Softy Mikes?" Dave said, mainly to himself.

Before they had made this journey Dave had known there was a reason why he should be here on the island of Maiti, though he hadn't known what it was at the time. But he did — now.

"I don't know Dave," Tariq replied unhappily. "But we need to do something, don't we?"

"Of course we do Tariq. It is clear, now, that this is the reason we came here; destiny has guided us." Dave had started talking in his serious voice. "We have to make sure the children of the world get the toys they asked for from Santa, as long as they have been good of course. Not just the ones they are given." Dave now fully understood the gut feeling he'd had back in England, and the reason he'd promised Tariq that using his 'fast skill' was the right thing to do.

"What should we do now?"

"What we do now — is wait and watch," Dave explained. "As long as DJ Wrapper, also known as Santa Claus as we now know, is doing his stuff then we can be sure that, when the time comes, he will be off in his sleigh delivering the right presents to the right kids. If there are any changes to his plans we will know he has been got at. But we only have nine days to do it."

"Tremendous," said Tariq.

Chapter 26.
EV1L-5A/NTA

During the course of their conversation, Gene Baubs had been told of his boss's plan.

"Gene," Gilbert Bates said. "Just to make sure you understand what I'm telling you I'll say it again."

"Okay, sir," Gene replied, happy that he would get a second chance at understanding his boss's intentions.

"Firstly, Gene, we'll have to replace DJ Wrapper with someone we can rely on."

"How will we do that?"

"It's just a short call to someone back at my offices."

"What about the cuddly toys?" Gene said.

"That's another short call to another office," Gilbert Bates replied.

"What will the cuddly toys look like?"

"They will be bears, of a beige colour, with glasses just like mine. And they will also be soft and have a name stitched into one of their ears," Gil said finally as he finished explaining his plan.

"What name would that be, sir?" Gene asked in a hushed tone as he leant over their table towards his boss.

Gilbert Bates leant towards his PA and whispered a single word, "Mike," he said. They both sat back in their chairs nodding at each other; then, Gene frowned.

"If you don't mind me saying so, sir; those bears you've described are quite like every other soft and cuddly bear."

"No, Gene, I don't mind you saying so. This is why my plan is so good. The difference will be that, in each and every one of my bears, there will be a radio frequency computer chip designed to program the minds of children, and their parents, telling them that my Softy Mike toy will be the only toy they will want for Christmas — and **forever**!" Gilbert Bates paused for a moment letting his idea sink in. "My research department has been working on this technology for a long time and it's now ready to be used."

"That's incredibly brilliant, sir."

"Of course it is, Gene and not only that," Gil continued divulging the details, "the computer chip will also make them want accessories for the Softy Mike, accessories that only my company will be selling, such things as clothing for the bears, houses for the bears and toy banks for the bears." Gilbert Bates was smiling an evil smile again.

"Wow!" Gene said, now understanding his boss's intentions. Then his brow furrowed as another question came to him. "How will you get Santa to hand out your Softy Mikes?"

"That's very simple my dear PA, the Santa we know — won't."

"Isn't that bad?" Gene said.

"Yes and no," Gil replied, smiling his evil grin once more, and not being able to help himself, he started rubbing his hands together for the third time this holiday.

Gene was curious; he had no idea as to how his boss would get Santa to deliver the Softy Mike toys and nothing else. But before he could ask Gilbert Bates to explain the last bit of his plan, Gil began to tell him.

"Gene, we will replace Mr DJ Wrapper with an exact duplicate, a machine that behaves and acts exactly like DJ Wrapper, but will be under our control, through mobile telephone technology!"

"Where will you get that from, sir?" Gene asked, hoping his boss would not be annoyed by yet another question from a lowly PA. But his boss wasn't unhappy; he was pleased he would be able to explain.

"I will make a phone call to my Research and Development department and ask for the EV1L 5A/NTA unit they have been working on." Gilbert Bates was glad that the ideas he'd had for the future growth of his company were not wasted; though he was surprised he'd got a chance to use one of them while he was on holiday.

Before he had left for the Island of Maiti, his R&D department had sent him a report that had told him his Experimental Vehicle, 1st Level, 5th series Android/Nano-Technology Automaton was ready. This piece of machinery was known as EV1L 5A/NTA for short.

He dialled the number to his research labs from his mobile phone and told them that the EV1L 5A/NTA unit they'd been developing needed to be delivered, immediately, to his holiday apartment on the Island of Maiti; the day after tomorrow, at the very latest; because if it wasn't they could start looking for new jobs straightaway. As soon as he'd finished telling the scientists from his R&D department, what they should be doing, Gilbert Bates turned off his phone and put it back in his pocket.

He turned to his PA. "Gene," he said smiling, "the replacement Santa will be here in two days."

Chapter 27.
Flip-Flops and Pink Sunglasses

On the morning following the dance show, Dave and Tariq got up early; they now had a mission to make sure that Santa, after he had finished his day job, the one he did when he wasn't flying around the world delivering presents, would be able to get on and deliver those presents without any interference from the people Tariq had overheard the night before.

Dave, putting on his flip-flops, and Tariq putting on his pink clam shell sunglasses left their chalet very early, making their way to the breakfast bar. They needed to seek out the two people Tariq had heard plotting DJ Wrapper's demise, thus removing any chance that the good children of the world would get the presents they deserved at Christmas.

After two hours of toying with the food they had ordered for their morning meal, Tariq spotted the two individuals he'd heard discussing the replacement of all Santa's presents the evening before.

"Dave! There they are," Tariq said pointing at, Gene Baubs and Gilbert Bates as they arrived in the breakfast bar.

"Okay Tariq," Dave said. "Act normal and watch them."

"Right you are, Dave."

The morning went on and nothing much more happened. The two individuals finished their breakfast, got up and walked back to their apartment. Dave and Tariq moved from their seats in the breakfast bar and followed closely behind, but not too closely. When the two men had entered their apartment, Dave and Tariq found an appropriate place to hide and watch from.

After 30 minutes, Gene Baubs and Gilbert Bates left the apartment dressed in different clothing, but not the type of clothing usually associated with masters of evil plans. Unless they were being very clever, it looked to Dave that all they were going to do was spend the rest of the day on the beach.

Dave and Tariq changed their position from the Hibiscus bush they had been hiding in, to a bar that had been built out over the small bay which fronted the Royal DeMacaroon holiday resort. Sitting down on two swing seats, seats that were suspended from the ceiling of the brightly coloured bar, Tariq ordered a lettuce smoothie for himself.

"Sorry, Mon," the bartender said. "Dis bar jus serve de fruit juice, Mon."

"Okay," Tariq said, a little disappointed. "I'll have two fruit juices then. Thank you." Just as he turned away he had another thought. "I don't suppose you do lettuce ice cream, do you?"

"Sure, Mon. All sorts of ice cream."

Tariq began to smile and collected a couple of ice creams to go with the fruit juices.

Enjoying the sun, Dave and Tariq supped their drinks and licked their ice creams whilst they watched and waited. Tariq had decided to get Dave a vanilla one. He didn't think Dave would have liked the special flavour of lettuce ice cream.

*

The two individuals that were, Gene Baubs and Gilbert Bates remained on their towels on the beach, soaking up the sun. Come one o'clock one of the two people, the one without the round gold rimmed glasses, opened up a hamper and started to dish out all sorts of sandwiches, putting them on white paper plates. When the meal was finished everything was put away again and the two people lay back down on their towels to take in the rest of the day's sun.

Still Dave and Tariq watched and waited, ready to stop the two men, as and when they decided to follow through with their plan to get rid of DJ Wrapper. But nothing happened. Dave and Tariq didn't know that Gilbert Bates could not follow through with his plan until the EV1L 5A/NTA unit had been delivered.

As the sun started its journey towards the horizon the two individuals, Tariq and Dave had been watching all day, packed up their hamper and beach towels and left the sandy cove.

"Well," said Dave.

"Well," Tariq repeated.

"There's not a lot going on here is there?"

"I think you're right about that Dave."

"Did you really hear them saying that they would have to replace Santa?"

"Of course I did," Tariq replied. "Trust me, I'm a tortoise."

"If you say so Tariq, not that I think you're not a tortoise of course. I can tell. You've a shell and a wrinkly neck."

"Thanks for that Dave! A wrinkly neck doesn't mean anything. Anyway I'm only 87 you know."

"EIGHTY-SEVEN!"

"Yes. What's wrong with that?" Tariq replied, a little offended at the way Dave had said *eighty-seven!*

"Eighty-seven," Dave repeated.

"And?"

"No. You're right Tariq. I suppose it's not that old for a tortoise."

"Of course it's not. I'm just a youngster."

Dismissing the subject Dave said, "I think it's best we leave."

Dave and Tariq left the bar over the sea and made their way back to their chalet. It seemed obvious to them that nothing special was going to happen for the remainder of the day, and as it was beginning to get dark they could turn in early for the evening. Then Dave had an idea.

"Tariq, this is the Island of Maiti isn't it?"

"Yes Dave, of course it is."

"Didn't it say in your book on Maiti that this island had shamans, you know what I mean — witch doctors," Dave said struggling to recall the words Tariq's book had used. "People who are fortune-tellers."

"Yes. What about them?"

"Well, if we could find one perhaps we could ask for some advice…… something that may give us the upper-hand when we need to thwart those dastardly evil-doers."

"Good idea Dave. Where do we find one of them, then?"

Dave pondered the question; hand on chin, resting his elbow on his other arm, which crossed his chest. Still thinking he stood in the middle of the path to their chalet, bolt upright, chin still resting on the thumb and forefinger of his hand. Using his toes he turned around on the spot looking for inspiration, and then he found it. Dave pointed towards the furthest end of the path they were standing on, and then marched off in the direction of his pointing finger. Tariq frowned, shrugged, and decided it might be a good idea to follow.

Dave stopped abruptly and announced, "We're here."

Tariq looked around and couldn't help noticing that, apart from the bushes and palm trees and another path, there wasn't really that much to see.

"Where?"

"At the beginning of the path to the final destination which, when we reach it, will be where the shaman will also be."

"How do you know that Dave? Is it your TAP ability?" Tariq said, shaking his head in wonder at his friend's amazing abilities.

"No," Dave said, pointing to the signpost he had stopped in front of.

On it there were four signs, each one pointing in a different direction. The first said, '*Club Extravaganza*' in brackets it also said, '*(Entertainments complex)*', the second read, '*Pool*' and in brackets it had, '*(Swimming)*', the third pointed in another direction and also read, '*Pool*' and in brackets it had, '*(snooker, billiards, cricket and other ball and stick games, room)*'. The last and most important sign for Dave and Tariq read, '*To the Temple of Yoodoo*', this finger post didn't have anything extra written on it, not even brackets.

"This way," Dave said and started walking in the direction of the Temple of Yoodoo with Tariq strolling beside him.

The path took them out of the Royal DeMacaroon Club Carib resort and after about five minutes of walking it turned from a pavement into a loamy dirt track which was lined, either side, by more Hibiscus bushes and other varieties of plant. As they made their way further and further along the path the route to the Temple of Yoodoo became darker, large Coconut trees and Florida palms growing on each side of it, the tops touching and creating a canopy over the dirt track. Occasionally they caught glimpses of monkey-like animals, hopping silently from tree top to tree top. They were now in the deep jungle and the sun was about to disappear for the night, as it had a Top Trumps evening to attend.

"Dave, it's getting really dark now. Where do you think we are?"

"Don't worry Tariq. We're on the path to the Temple of Yoodoo — in the deep jungle."

"I was afraid you were going to say that. How much further do we have to go?"

Dave looked at his finger; it was still pointing forwards. Then Dave looked at where it was pointing.

"There," Dave said, pointing at some flickering candles outlining a white painted wooden door, which was cleverly placed beneath a sign declaring, '*The Temple of Yoodoo*'

The temple seemed to be made from the very jungle itself, with reddy-orange coloured mud walls rising from the soil. Its roof was made from, obviously ancient, long-stemmed grasses that all looked like they'd just been dumped on top of the cone-shaped roof when it had been built. It was at the centre of a small clearing in the deep jungle, trees soaring into the night sky around it, with a well-trodden path leading either side of the round walled building.

Dave walked up to the temple's door and knocked, after a long pause a heavily accented deep voice spoke out, it seemed to come from the depths of the jungle itself.

"Oo is it dat, dat come seek de advice of de priest of de temple of Yoodoo, me old china plates?"

Dave nodded at Tariq and smiled. "See," he whispered.

"See what?" Tariq whispered back.

"This is the place to come; even before the high priest has opened the door, he knows we've come for advice."

Tariq saw what Dave was getting at and mouthed "Wow!"

"It is I, Dave," Dave started to explain, "Dave the Feather and my dear friend, Tariq the Tortoise of the Insomniacs."

Tariq elbowed Dave.

"Tariq the Gifted, that is," Dave added quickly.

The door they were standing in front of opened slowly inwards showing a dim flickering interior; smells from incense and even more burning candles, seeped out into the night sky, and passed through Dave's and Tariq's nostrils. The two friends entered the hut.

Sitting in a wooden chair, opposite a wall covered with hundreds of burning candles, was a very tall black man in dazzling white robes with a fluffy grey-white beard sprouting from his chin, who welcomed them in.

"Ah!" the High Priest of the Temple of Yoodoo said, as Dave and Tariq came into the flickering light.

"Ah." Dave and Tariq nodded back.

"Ow ca mi 'elp fi yu, me manhole covers?" the High Priest asked in his booming voice.

"Well...," Dave began.

"Yuh ha' Barney Rubbles wid dem blackheart mans?" the priest observed.

"Yes and..."

"'Ol' on." The priest raised his hand and Dave stopped speaking. The priest then reached beneath his chair and grabbed an earthenware flask full of liquid. "Tretch out yuh Jazz bands, me old china," the priest instructed.

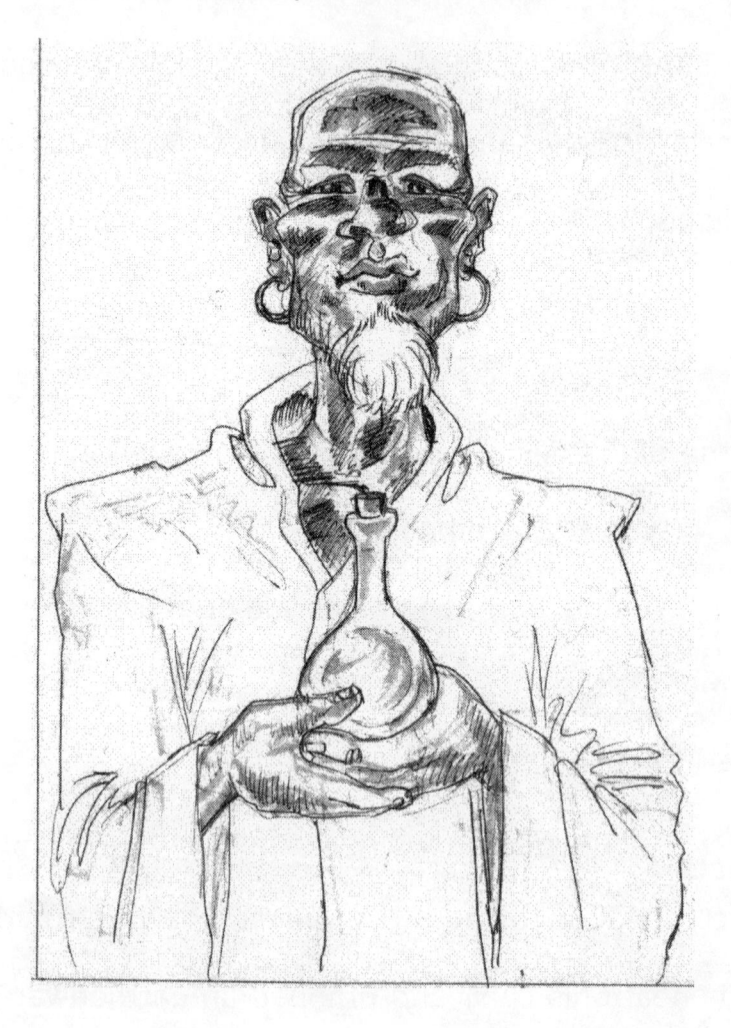

Dave stretched both his hands out towards the priest and the man in the white robes placed the flask in them.

"Dis is de juice of de Temple of Yoodoo," the priest began as he stood up, his head nearly touching the ceiling. "Yu use dis as yu do, when de time is right. Seen?"

"Er — yes," Dave said, "and, thank you."

"Dis juice work only if yu Adam and Eve it," the priest warned, and pointed to the door.

"Right... and thanks again." Dave turned to Tariq, "I think it's time to go."

The pair left the temple and the door gradually swung shut of its own accord behind them, as if driven by magic. Just before it finished closing the priest's booming voice reached their ears one final time. "One Love" the priest said, then the door was shut and the candles that covered the outside of the temple snuffed themselves out.

Dave was left holding an earthen flask containing some kind of liquid, and Tariq was staring, in a worried kind of way, at the complete darkness that now surrounded them.

"Dave, how are we going to get back in the dark?"

"TAP."

"Tremendous," said Tariq, and Dave led the way back to the resort.

Chapter 28.
A Delivery

As the sun silently rose the next morning from behind the edge of the deep blue sea into the cloudless sky, the quietness of the early morning was suddenly shattered by a thumping on the door of Baubs and Bates's apartment.

Gil rolled over in his bed, opening his eyes slightly. "GENE." he yelled, "There's someone at the door; can you find out who it is?"

"Wahh?" Gene said as he was suddenly brought out of his sleep by Gil's voice.

"GENE, get the door."

"Of course, sir. No problem, sir. The door will be dealt with very shortly..., sir."

Gene got out of bed, put on his lilac silk dressing gown and crossed the apartment, opening the door to their room.

"Dis for you Mon," the man at the door said.

"Eh?" Gene answered.

"Dis packet. It for you, Mon," the man explained further.

"Sorry, I don't quite understand."

The delivery man shrugged his shoulders, then putting on an American accent he said, "Good morning, sir. I have a package for you; if you will take it."

"Ah!" Gene replied, now comprehending what he was being told. "Where do I sign?"

"Jus here, Mon," the man said indicating the place on the delivery note.

"Eh?" Gene replied.

Oh Jah! the delivery man thought. *Why is it I always get dese people?* Then he said, "Sir, if you would kindly sign right here I will be able to leave you with this package I have delivered."

"Thank you very much; and please take this as an appreciation of your service." Gene handed the man a twenty dollar bill after signing the delivery note.

"Tanks, Mon." The man took the bill and left before any other conversation could take place.

Gene shrugged once again wondering why the delivery person had left so promptly and then manoeuvred the large cardboard encased package into the apartment.

Chapter 29.
Bobboggs and Bungle-bees

Dave was already awake when his alarm went off; he'd not had a very good night's sleep because the night had been clear and the moon had been out. It wasn't that the clear night had made any noise to keep him awake, and certainly the moonbeams had been pretty quiet as well; it was, in fact, the weird monkey-like animals that inhabited the island who had been responsible for the strange noises throughout the night.

"What in the blue skies of earth was that racket last night?" Dave asked Tariq. "I hardly got a wink of sleep. It was like an awful version of DJ Wrapper's show."

"It was the Bobboggs Dave."

"How d'you know that?"

"I didn't at first, but after a while, and because I couldn't concentrate on putting the final touches to my most excellent culinary delight of lettuce custard, I looked it up in one of the books I brought with me," Tariq explained. "They only come out to sing on clear nights when the moon is full, mimicking the sounds of the island. I think we saw them in the jungle last night."

"Mimicking the sounds of the island! Singing, indeed!"

"I don't think there's much that can be done about it — but perhaps......" Tariq drifted off, thinking.

"But perhaps what?" Dave asked.

"Perhaps I could convert my tortoise nose bungs into some kind of feather ear plug."

Dave shuddered at the thought. "Don't worry Tariq. I'm sure I'll get used to it." He checked the time, "I think we ought to be getting ready to continue our observations of those master criminals you discovered the other day — we can't let anything happen to Santa on our watch. This is what we're here for."

Dave and Tariq got ready to stake-out the evil-doers' apartment, it was still early enough for them not to have left for breakfast yet.

"Tariq, bring your satchel," Dave said. "We made need it."

After placing the flask from the Temple of Yoodoo in his satchel, Tremendous Tariq the Tortoise and Brave Dave the Feather snuck out of their chalet, making their way to the ground-level apartment of, Gene Baubs and Gilbert

Bates. As they wandered through the resort, towards Baubs and Bates's apartment, they began to hear another very strange sound drifting towards them through the still morning air, of the island.

Bzzzzz, schtuma, bzzzzz, schtuma, bzzzzz, schtuma — oops

Dave and Tariq looked at each other not knowing what to make of it. They listened again.

Bzzzzz, schtuma, bzzzzz, schtuma, bzzzzz, schtuma — oops

"What *is* that? Do you know, Tariq?"

"No, but hold on though...... I've brought my *Encyclopaedia of Maiti Flora and Fauna*." Tariq said, diving into his shell to retrieve the book.

He flicked through the pages quickly, "Ah! Here it is."

"And what is it?" Dave asked.

"It's a bungle-bee — another native creature; related to our bumblebees back home."

"Is that all your book says?"

"No, apparently the bungle-bee is a fairly new species and it has evolved a kind of audio camouflage which fits in with the nation's preferred music genre."

"You mean Reggae?"

"Yep."

"What's the '*oops*' about then?"

"Its vision is not very good because it has evolved an audio-centric nature and, according to the book, it navigates its environment by touch."

"You don't mean by bumping into things do you?" Dave said shaking his head at the thought.

"That's what it says here."

"I hope it doesn't bump into me," Dave said. "Does it have a sting?"

"The encyclopaedia says it does, but mostly it can't be bothered to use it."

"That's *good*. I mean, you're okay you've got a shell, all I've got is my fancy yellow body suit."

"You've got the Concretonator suit as well." Tariq reminded Dave.

"That's a point, but as the bungle-bee is unlikely to sting I'll save it for emergencies. Shhh now Tariq, we're almost outside the evil-doers' apartment."

They tiptoed up to a rather large Hibiscus plant and stepped into its centre. It was opposite the door of the apartment. Pulling back its huge green leaves and branches they peered out, staring at the curtain covered windows to the apartment, hoping to catch a glimpse of what was going on inside. They were now in place and had started their second day's stake-out of the wrong-doers to be. One way or another Dave and Tariq were going to find out what the master criminal's dastardly plan was.

Chapter 30.
Robot Flat Packs

Gene Baubs mopped the sweat from his brow; the package was certainly very heavy. "What do you want me to do with this package, sir?"

"Put it in the corner for a moment and order some breakfast to be delivered," Gil said.

"Right away, sir." Gene shifted the package into the corner of their room and as soon as he was finished he called reception to order their breakfast. Within 15 minutes there was a knock at the door and their breakfast had arrived.,

Gene tipped the young woman who had brought their food and took the meal to the table in the room.

When they had both finished eating Gil said, "Now we can get on with the rest of my plan."

"We certainly can, sir," Gene replied.

"First, Gene, you need to unpack the EV1L 5A/NTA unit and assemble it."

"Absolutely, sir."

"After that we will test it. My mobile phone has the controls for the unit built into it."

"Yes, sir."

"And, Gene?"

"Yes, sir?"

"Can you hurry up and put it together. I don't pay you to dawdle do I?"

"Yes, sir, I mean, no, sir."

Gene Baubs removed all the packaging and placed the parts of the EV1L 5A/NTA unit on the floor. The pieces of the machinery looked familiar; arms, legs and feet being obvious. It seemed to, Gene that building the robot would be a fairly straightforward task. But, not wanting to fail his boss, he removed the sealed instructions for assembling the machine. After looking through them for a moment he started to put the parts together using the tool kit that had been provided as part of the delivered package.

Four hours later, Gene put the tools down. The machine was now complete, in a way, and as it sat on a chair, it looked almost Santa like. It had the red velvet clothing; it had the same red velvet flip-flops, Gene had seen DJ Wrapper wearing the other night. There were only slight differences between the real Santa and this robot version. The machine's face had, under a wiry white beard, cheeks and a chin that were a little more square than they ought to be, and its eyes had a strange multi-coloured look about them.

"Sir, it's done…… Well sort of."

"What do you mean 'sort of'?" Gilbert Bates demanded.

"Well... I've followed the instructions and there seems to be some bits left over." Gene pointed to the pile of screws, wires and circuit boards that now covered the centre of the main table in their apartment.

"Gene, have you followed the instructions exactly?"

"Yes," Gene replied.

"Are you certain that you have followed everything in the instructions?" Gil asked once more.

"Yes," Gene replied once again.

"If you're happy that you have followed them exactly then those parts left over must be spares," Gil said.

"Yes, sir," Gene said. He couldn't actually say anything else if he was going to keep on his boss's good side.

"Okay, I'll start it up using the special jog dial I've had installed in my mobile phone."

Gilbert Bates pressed the jog dial inwards and the EV1L 5A/NTA unit's eyes lit up, cycling through the primary colours of blue, red and green as it booted-up, finally finishing on yellow, which wasn't one of the primary colours where adding different coloured lights together was concerned, that is, yellow wasn't one of the additive primary colours. He was happy, and seeing the machine his R&D department had created begin to work, he clapped his hands with glee, and then started rubbing them against each other. He loved it when a plan came together.

Chapter 31.
Stiff Legs and Evil Beach Bags

During Dave and Tariq's vigil in the large leafed, dark green Hibiscus plant, the one that was growing outside of the master criminal's apartment, they'd seen a breakfast delivered; heard nothing for a while, then listened to some banging and bashing sounds coming from behind the door to the evil-doers' apartment, for four hours or more. Neither of them had any idea what was going on.

"What d'you think is going on Dave?"

"I don't know Tariq. But you can rest assured that it is something quite dastardly and evil, if I'm a feather who's fallen from a large bird not so many weeks ago."

"But you *are* a feather and you *did* fall from a bird," Tariq replied. Not quite understanding what Dave was saying.

"Exactly," Dave said, knowingly.

Tariq decided to leave that particular conversation as it was, there was too much going on to consider; rather than getting bogged down in Dave's apparent non-answer.

Midday came and went and apart from a few crashes from the apartment, not a lot more happened. Dusk began to set and Dave began to worry that they'd not been watching the right apartment, and if that was the case then Santa was in grave danger.

"Tariq, are you really sure that these are the two people you heard talking about getting rid of all of Santa's presents?"

"Dave, if my name was not Tariq of the Insomniacs, Tariq the Gifted that is, then I would understand your doubt. But it is, and I am, and I know what I heard and in hearing it, it was apparent. Because if I didn't, then I wouldn't have, and we wouldn't be here now — but I did," Tariq said, explaining his point as clearly as he could to Dave.

Before Dave could answer they both heard the door to the master criminals' apartment creak slowly open, in the dimming light. Dave and Tariq peered out, pulling back a few of the Hibiscus plant's leaves so they could see more clearly what was going on in the gradually darkening early November evening.

Two people left the room and started to make their way to the resort's entertainment complex; one of them was carrying a large and evil looking red beach bag decorated with a floral design consisting of small white daisy-like flowers — *and* it was full to the brim with something, but neither Tariq nor Dave, could make out what exactly was in it. By the way the evil-doers walked Dave knew that the next steps he and Tariq would have to take were going to be very important indeed; especially if they were going to thwart the plan Tariq had overheard the two individuals discussing two nights before.

"Oh Dear," said Dave as an idea popped into his head in a flash of inspiration.

"Why 'Oh Dear' Dave?" Tariq asked, a little uneasy by the way Dave had said, *'Oh Dear'.*

"I think I've worked out how those people are going to get Santa to give out *only* the toy bears."

"How's that Dave?"

"They're going to change him," Dave said, frowning at the thought.

"Wow — put some different clothes on him; does it really make that much difference?"

"No Tariq; they're going to keep the clothes but just change the person in them."

"No Dave, they can't do that — it can't be so." Tariq said in a cry of despair that was almost too loud.

The door to the apartment opposite them creaked once again as it seemingly closed by itself.

"I believe it has started Tariq. The fact that the two dastardly individuals have left the building and the fact that we know there was probably something being built in the apartment because of the noises we heard today, means we're going to have to split up. We can't be in two places at once."

"You mean you have to go somewhere and I also have to go somewhere other than where you're going?" Tariq asked, hoping beyond hope he had *not* understood correctly what Dave was saying.

"This is what is generally meant by splitting up Tariq," Dave said confirming his friend's worry, in his ongoing serious tone.

"What d'you want to do?" Dave said. "Stay here and continue to watch the apartment or follow those two dastardly criminals, one of which is carrying a particularly evil looking red bag?"

Tariq wasn't too keen on the idea of following a pair of dastardly criminals particularly as the one in the cloak seemed to have very stiff legs and might be a little cross if approached; and as the apartment was now empty, barring a hammer that he supposed he had heard bashing something earlier, he made his decision.

"Dave, I'll stay here and watch the apartment, because if anything truly sinister and evil is going to happen it will be here," he said, knowing full well that the apartment was empty and it was quite unlikely that anything further evil and sinister was going to happen.

"Okay Tariq, I think you've made a brave choice," Dave said, meaning it.

"Have I?" Tariq replied, startled by Dave's response. He was now unsure as to whether he had made the right choice, but he was also unsure, why it wasn't.

"You have, Tariq. You *are* a brave tortoise."

Tariq gulped and in a jittering voice replied, "O, o, o, o, okay. I'll catch up with you later. — Won't I?"

"Of course you will. Shame we haven't got any way to keep in contact with each other. If anything goes wrong we'll meet at the bar over the water in five hours. Make sure you wear a pink carnation, I'll do the same; in this way we'll be able to recognise each other." Dave explained how the next few hours were going to be, continuing in the same serious tone he'd been using since they'd decided to watch and observe the master criminals that Tariq had discovered.

"Bye Tariq."

"You going then?" Tariq asked, very worried.

"Yes. I'm off to follow those people. And chin up Tariq, keep out of trouble, you hear me?"

"I, I, I, I," Tariq started, then finished, "I will." He was barely able to get the words out because he was so afraid.

Dave patted him on the shoulder. "Don't worry Tariq. Whether I live or die I'm sure you will survive. See you in the next life, if not before."

Tariq's chin almost hit the floor on hearing what Dave had just said. He had already forgotten the advice to keep his chin up.

Dave winked. "Sorry Tariq. Couldn't resist that. I was only joking."

"Thanks Dave, that's just tremendous," Tariq moaned as Dave sneaked off to follow the two people they'd seen leave the apartment.

Once Dave had disappeared out of sight Tariq sat down in the centre of the dark green leafed Hibiscus plant to watch the now apparently empty apartment. Nothing was stirring and through the window to the wrong-doers' room nothing could be seen as it was now completely dark.

Chapter 32.
A Floppy Hat and Nice Tights

Gilbert Bates was walking quite fast as he made his way to the resort's restaurant. He wanted to get himself a table next to the stage where DJ Wrapper would be performing his evening gig. A wobbly man in a large hooded cloak followed him, struggling to keep up. The man walked in an almost mechanical manner, stiff legs flicking out one in front of the other. It was as if he had just learnt to walk that very evening and had no idea what his knees were for. But Gilbert Bates took no notice of his apparent friend's ambulatory problem. He didn't care how the person walked, just that he was able to do it. He only needed him for the duration of his dastardly plan.

As they walked into the resort's restaurant Gilbert Bates spied a suitable table, it was next to the DJ's dressing room and quite close to the stage as well. Timing was crucial if his plan was to work. He had to make sure that when the time came it was his EV1L 5A/NTA machine that got up onto the stage instead of the DJ, who at a certain time of the year became Santa Claus, just for one night.

Gilbert Bates had decided he would distract the man in red as soon as he had left his dressing room, and certainly while the lights were still dim, and persuade Mr. Claus, somehow, to go into the empty storeroom behind the stage. After that he would lock Mr. Claus in, until he could get him off the Isle of Maiti and back to his offices in New York. If he timed this just right no one would notice the swap.

Gilbert Bates was certain that it would only take him one Christmas to make sure all the children in the entire world (and their parents) were under his control, only wanting to buy his Softy Mike toys and, of course, their accessories. After that he could think about letting Santa go or, perhaps, getting rid of him for good.

Sitting down at the table he signalled to his new friend to do the same. The dancers, who were already on stage, were about to finish their routine and very shortly the lights would dim and then the stagehands would get up onto the stage and change the set ready for DJ Wrapper. This was the time when he would act.

Gilbert Bates leant over the table and adjusted his partner's cloak, he didn't want anyone to notice who his partner looked like.

"Get ready," Gilbert Bates instructed.

"Affirmative, sir," the cloaked accomplice replied, in a slightly metallic voice.

The dancers left the stage and the lights went out plunging the entertainments area into darkness. The audience, pleased with what they had seen, began to applaud. Soon the clapping died away and one by one the audience got up from their seats and made their way to the bar to get some refreshments before the next part of the show started.

Gilbert Bates was watching DJ Wrapper's dressing room door very carefully and as it began to open he got up from his chair. Quickly he made his way to the dressing room and once outside Gilbert Bates signalled to his accomplice. His cloaked friend stood up, waiting in the shadows, for the next instructions from its master.

"Excuse me," Gilbert Bates said, standing in the doorway, as DJ Wrapper attempted to leave his dressing room.

"Er! Yes Sonny?" DJ Wrapper said, a little startled.

"I have someone you may want to meet."

"I'm sorry Sonny, I don't have the time at the moment, but after my set there will be plenty."

"I have someone you need to meet Mister DJ Wrapper — or is it...... Santa Claus! If I'm not mistaken?" Gilbert Bates said evilly.

"Ho, ho, ho... I think you have the wrong person Sonny," DJ Wrapper said, not quite stating the exact truth, attempting to keep his true identity secret; knowing that it was only on occasions like this he should not speak the complete truth of the matter. If everyone found out what he did for a job the rest of the time it would be impossible to do his Christmas job in the way it should be done.

"No, no, no... I don't think I do."

"Sonny, I appreciate what you're saying, but you are truly mistaken," Santa continued, saying anything he could to keep his real identity from becoming known.

"So…… The fact of your floppy red velvet headwear means nothing?"

"It's just my gig sonny," Santa replied.

"And your red velvet overcoat with fluffy white trimmings means nothing?"

"Nothing at all," DJ Wrapper answered.

"And the fact that your flip-flops have white fluffy pom-poms on has no bearing on who you are?"

Santa was getting very worried now. "What do you want, sonny? Because you're not going to get it."

"Am I not — Mister Santa Claus?" Gilbert Bates said using DJ Wrapper's real name once again.

"Ah!" Santa said, knowing his disguise had been penetrated. If only he'd liked the type of clothing that didn't just happen to be red or have fluffy white trimmings, perhaps he would have got away with pretending to be someone else.

"Santa, you can come with me now and accept the situation or — suffer the consequences." Gilbert Bates threatened.

"You won't win sonny, whoever you are. I am Santa Claus and Santa Claus always wins," he replied firmly.

Gilbert Bates started to laugh his evil little laugh. What a stupid thing for Santa to say. Gilbert Bates always got what he wanted. He waved towards the shadows that surrounded his table and out of the dark stepped the cloak covered electric EV1L 5A/NTA machine. DJ Wrapper looked at it, stunned, knowing he had been rumbled.

"You think I won't win Mister DJ, but you're wrong, I will." Gilbert Bates pointed to his robot.

"My people won't fall for it."

"We'll see about that," Gilbert Bates said. "Please follow me."

"And if I don't?"

Gilbert Bates pressed a few buttons on his mobile phone and the EV1L 5A/NTA machine pointed at a small plate on the table. There was a brief flash of lime green light from the cloaked person's finger tips and the plate crumbled into a pile of dust.

"Oh! Oh! Oh!" Santa said grimly. "I'll follow you. But you won't get away with this, you know."

"You think I won't, Santa, but I already am!" Gilbert Bates answered, cackling to himself.

Pressing a few more buttons on his mobile phone, the robotic Santa pulled its cloak off to reveal its dress. The robot stood there in the dark, looking exactly like DJ Wrapper, apart from a squarish face and a pair of strangely yellow eyes.

Gilbert Bates typed another number into his phone and then put it to his ear and began to speak. "Baubs... get here now." He turned his phone off and put it back in his pocket.

*

Tariq had got quite bored watching the empty apartment and as nothing had happened he'd decided to go back into his shell to see if there was anything else he could do, to make his lettuce custard even better than it already was. He wondered whether the Dunn's River Everyday Seasoning he'd found in their holiday chalet would give his custard that extra special something, and as he didn't know, he decided to give it a try.

While Tariq was testing out the latest ingredient for his custard the door to the apartment he was supposed to be watching opened and, Gene Baubs left in a hurry to assist Gilbert Bates.

*

The lights on the stage were beginning to slowly brighten and it was almost time for DJ Wrapper to get up onto the stage and start his show.

Gilbert Bates led an unwilling Santa Claus to the empty storeroom in the seldom used corridor behind the stage and shoved him inside, slamming the door shut and locking it.

"Sir, you called," Gene said as he arrived.

"Yes, Gene. I need you to watch over Mister DJ Wrapper while I make sure everything else goes to plan. But before you do that, and to make sure none of Santa's little helpers interrupt, you'll have to become one of them."

"How will I do that, sir, if that's not an impertinent question?"

"No, Gene, it's not — Grab that red bag by the table will you?" Gilbert Bates pointed to the red bag with the white daisies on its side. They both walked back towards the table.

Gene Baubs picked the bag up. "This one?"

"Yes. That one. Pull all the clothes out and put them on as quickly as you can; there's not much time left. So hurry."

Gene pulled the clothes out one by one. There were some olive green tights, a pair of pointy black shoes with toes that curled at the end, a stripy red and white long sleeved top and a green velvet waistcoat. Before putting them on, Gene Baubs emptied his pockets onto the table; there wasn't much in them, just his mobile phone. As he finished putting on the new clothes there was only one thing left in the bag. Pulling out the floppy green and pointed hat, he placed it on his head. He looked like, what could only be described as, an overly tall and skinny Elf.

Gene Baubs dumped the empty bag on the table, on top of his phone, and although he was ready he wasn't quite sure what he was meant to do. However, he did like the feel of the tights all the same.

"Excellent, Gene," his boss told him. "Now stand outside that door over there and make sure our guest does not leave." He pointed to the storeroom he had locked Santa in and after a moment's thought he added, "And make sure none of his little friends get in. Okay? If they turn up that is."

"Yes, sir… What little friends?"

"If you see anyone who looks like you, but a little shorter, tell them you're Santa's new chief Elf and he can't be disturbed. Then tell them to go back to Lapland, or wherever it is they come from. And make sure the toys for Christmas are the right ones."

"Yes, sir... Anything Elf?" Gene asked.

"Are you trying to be funny with me, Gene? Because if you are..."

"No, sir, of course not, sir." Gene said, regretting his little attempt at a joke.

"Good... Just make sure Santa, also known as DJ Wrapper, does not leave that room."

"Absolutely, you can count on me, sir."

"I hope I can, Gene," Gilbert Bates said sternly, "because if I can't...!" He left, Gene to fill in the blanks.

The stage lights were almost turned up to their full brightness and Gilbert Bates turned towards his creation. "Robot — get on that stage. NOW," Gilbert Bates commanded.

"Affirmative, sir," the EV1L 5A/NTA machine said, and stumbled up the short steps onto the stage, behind DJ Wrapper's turntables, on its stiff legs.

*

Dave looked on astounded. He hadn't interrupted the angry conversation between one of the dastardly evil-doers and DJ Wrapper because he'd had to make sure the real Santa would not come to any harm, before he made his move.

*

As the lights lit up the stage the audience began to applaud and, as the robot version of DJ Wrapper started spinning the discs, there was a bright flash followed by a huge clap of thunder, which cracked through the night sky above the Royal DeMacaroon Club Carib resort. The other type of Caribbean weather, the *not* sunny type, in fact the type that was wet, windy, very loud, and occasionally very bright, was beginning to make an appearance, as it tended to do at this time of year.

The audience hadn't noticed that their beloved DJ had been swapped for something that was almost but not quite DJ Wrapper. They also didn't know that the original DJ Wrapper was in fact the original Santa Claus.

The show started and over the top of the sounds blasting out from the bass cabinets of the sound system, the robot Santa started rapping.

"Whether black or white, your kids are cool.

"A Softy Mike will make them rule.

"Being Happy is a kiddies' right...

"and a Softy Mike will make them like to spennnnddd ... your —"

Before the electric Santa could utter the word '*money*' Gilbert Bates hit a button on his mobile phone to turn off the robot's voice. That was a close call he thought. When he got back to New York he would be having words with whoever had written the speech program for the electric Santa, the robot had nearly given the game away. He hoped there were no other glitches with his automaton.

The music carried on, pulsing into all those listening and no one seemed to notice that the fake DJ Wrapper had started a kind of miming rap. Perhaps the holidaymakers just thought it was a style of rapping that was silent, perhaps even a new style — one that had never been heard before.

*

On hearing the beats and the lyrics and then seeing the miming Dave knew it was now time to act, somehow he had to stop the evil-doers' plan from being completed.

*

Huge drops of rain started to fall from the night sky as the Caribbean storm edged its way over the holiday resort. The Bobboggs that had come to listen to the music once again, lifted palm fronds over their heads to fend off the worst of the downpour. Gradually the stars above the hotel winked out of existence as the storm clouds began to gather. Lightning flashed brightly through the night sky, each flash being followed by a booming clap of thunder.

The resort's staff appeared, as if from nowhere, and using longs sticks they began to pull out canvas canopies from their housings, making a roof above the open air stage. As the storm gathered strength, the air began to feel as if it had been electrified by its very presence.

*

Leaving, Gene to guard the door to the room Santa Claus was now in, Gilbert Bates snuck off in the deepening darkness of the storm. He needed to find somewhere where he could control the electric Santa without being seen and somewhere where he could continue his plan without being disturbed.

*

Dave left his position of safety at the table next to the bar, where he had been observing how the master criminals were going to complete their evil plan. He had seen the person with the small round spectacles use a mobile phone to control the robot Santa and when he reached the now empty table he noticed the red bag sitting on top of it. Looking around to make sure no one was watching him he picked the bag up and opened it, hoping there would be something inside, something that would help him figure out what the dastardly criminals were going to do next. To his disappointment it was empty. Shrugging off his despondency Dave was about to put the bag back, in exactly the same position, when he noticed a small object the red bag had been covering. He couldn't believe his luck. At the centre of the table was a mobile phone. Before making a grab for it he looked around once more, checking that no one was looking.

Nobody was looking at him, very carefully, and even *he* wasn't at all concerned with what Dave was about to do, as he thought it was probably the right thing to do in the circumstances. Everyone else still had their eyes on the stage watching the electric version of DJ Wrapper performing his silent rap in time with the loud music.

Dave grabbed the phone; this was going to be the way he would thwart the plan to replace Santa, a plan that was already underway. Putting what he thought was the mobile phone remote control unit into one of his impossibly deep pockets, he quickly walked away from the dastardly criminals' table and settled back down at his own, next to the juice bar. He knew the table he had picked had been a good choice since none of the guests at the resort sat near it. He hoped the fact that it was the only table not covered by the hastily erected canvas roofing, and therefore unprotected, would not make him stick out like slices of beetroot in a custard tart.

The rain poured over him but he didn't notice it, he'd never noticed rain in his entire life, it wasn't in his nature *to* notice it. He was, and had always been, waterproof. It was something he took for granted and never thought about. Whilst he sat there, with the drips rolling off him, Dave wondered what his next steps ought to be.

Chapter 33.
Lettuce Custard and Mobile Phones

Before tasting the latest version of his lettuce custard, Tariq thought it would be a good idea to take a peek at the apartment he was watching. Tariq replaced the lid of his saucepan and poked his head out of the top of his shell. He pulled back the leaves of the Hibiscus plant and looked at the master criminals' apartment. Nothing had changed. The rooms were still dark and no movement could be detected. Satisfied, Tariq dived back into his shell to continue the important culinary development of his custard. Taking the lid off the boiling liquid once more, he dipped in a spoon, and gingerly had a taste — it was certainly better than his first attempt he decided but, in his mind, it needed a little more *oomph*. Tariq looked around for other ingredients he could add.

*

Dave stared at the remote control he had managed to get hold of and thought, "Dis ting ain't wat it seems mi old china." Then he thought, "Oh no I've been here too long, I'm tinking in de local speak." Dave shook his head trying to focus on what he should be doing. He pressed a few buttons on the phone.

"The time sponsored by Accurist will be...," the phone barked, and before Dave could hear anything more meaningful the phone said, "zzzttttt," in time with a lightning flash. Then it continued. "Thirty seconds... beep, beep... zzzttttt." Another bolt of lightning streaked across the sky, followed by a huge *BOOM*.

He pressed a red button on the phone and the noises from it stopped. This was a much more complicated control device than he had ever imagined, and it seemed the storm was affecting it quite a lot. Another flash of lightning lit up the resort.

Chapter 34.
Text Message Rules

Gilbert Bates had found a small unused changing room next to the stage, whose doors were white and made up of small slats, ones which he could peek through and see his robot at work.

As the thunder boomed Gilbert Bates started writing the words his EV1L 5A/NTA would say next into his phone, ready to send the text message to his robot at the right moment.

He typed away, "AS A GIFT 2 ALL MY ADMIRERS I WILL GIVE U A TOY, A SOFTY MIKE. PLEASE COME UP 2 THE STAGE 2 RECEIVE IT. IT IS WHAT U DESERVE. THE SOFTY MIKE WILL NOT ONLY B GOOD 4 U BUT IT WILL ALSO B GOOD 4 UR KIDS AND UR GRANDKIDS. IF U DO NOT HAVE N E CHILDREN PLEASE THINK ABOUT THE CHILDREN U MAY HAVE IN THE FUTURE."

Gilbert Bates pressed a few more buttons on his phone and the electric Santa's voice was activated once again. He then pressed the send button and the message was sent to his robot. The counterfeit DJ Wrapper turned the music down and the audience hushed.

"As a gift to all my admirers," the electric DJ said. "I will give you a toy, a Softy Mike. Please come up to the stage to receive it. It is what you deserve. The Softy Mike will not only be good for you but it will also be good for your kids and your grandkids." The robot carried on, "If you do not have any children please think about the children you may have in the future."

One by one the audience began to queue up next to the electric DJ's turntables. From behind the huge speaker system the EV1L 5A/NTA robot retrieved a huge box of cuddly toys containing the specially made Radio Frequency Id computer chips and began to hand them out. As each and every one of the adults took the toy a glazed expression appeared on their faces. The RFID computer chips were beginning to do their work.

*

Dave was gradually getting closer to the fake DJ, desperately pressing any buttons he could find, hoping that at least one sequence on the phone would stop the robot from handing out anymore of the awful furry beige teddy bears. Nothing was happening and Dave was beginning to feel quite useless. Then all of a sudden his phone chirped into life.

"Hello, darling, what can I do for you tonight?" his phone said in a husky female voice.

"I need you to stop this evil robot," Dave said, glad that there had been some response from the phone.

"How would you like me... zzzttttt," the phone finished as yet another lightning bolt turned the night sky to white.

*

Gilbert Bates was so confident that his plan was working he left his little hidey hole, to get a better view of it in action. He laughed his evil laugh. "Har, ha, ha, har — ha." *I am so good*, he thought to himself, *I must be a genius, in fact I know I am*.

As he stepped out of the changing room into the open, holding his mobile phone remote control out in front of him, a dagger of light came from the sky and struck the phone. The force of the strike threw him back into his hiding place, unconscious, and the power surge caused a huge pulse of electricity to be sent into the EV1L 5A/NTA machine, overloading the robot's circuits.

*

Dave walked towards the stage, still pressing all sorts of buttons, one, two, three at a time, hoping he would hit the right combination very soon. All of a sudden the fake Santa stopped talking and started to dance in a very strange way. Dave pressed some more buttons and the fake Santa started to flick its arms, head and feet in ways a normal person couldn't. As this happened its dance got faster and faster until it was twirling around in a blur, its feet performing the first ever double speed, tap danced version of the *Coronation Street* theme tune.

In the blink of an eye the electric Santa started to knock over the speakers, it started knocking over the microphones and finally it knocked over the turntables as it turned and tumbled, jiggled and wiggled. Then it was on its own, lying on the floor, in the middle of the stage, flicking and twitching away to some kind of mental musical beat that no one could hear.

The audience didn't appreciate what they thought was a new part of DJ Wrapper's show and began to leave, very disappointed, to find something better to do. Those that had collected a Softy Mike still held on to the toy as if it was the best present they'd ever had.

There was another flash and another deep *BOOM*, as yet more lightning crashed across the night sky.

The robot Santa's light-bulb eyes suddenly blew outwards, yellowy steam pouring from them.

Dave continued pressing the buttons on the mobile phone, he knew he was on to a winner now and as the EV1L 5A/NTA machine collapsed onto the floor, each of the toys the robot had given out went *POOF* letting off a little bit of smoked from its chest, as the RFID chips were melted by the extra electricity coming from the out of control robot.

Those holidaymakers who had decided to have one of the toys, dropped their Softy Mikes onto the floor as each and every one of them heated up in their hands, finally bursting into small purpley-green flames seconds later. They no longer thought the toys were the best toys ever made and as they left the entertainments area to return to their apartments and chalets, a rather tall Elf-like person crept along the back of the now wrecked stage, hoping not to be noticed, calling quietly, "Sir, sir. Where are you?"

Chapter 35.
Hot Stuff

The *oomph* Tariq had expected from his new ingredient had turned out to be nothing he assumed the 'Dunn's River Everyday Seasoning' would be, but he hadn't used that much so he decided to empty the rest of the bottle into his lettuce custard mix and began to stir it again.

With any luck, he thought, *this ought to make some kind of difference.* He continued stirring.

Once the colour of the 'Dunn's River Seasoning' had disappeared and melted into the colour of his custard, he decided it was time to take another taste. This time he didn't ready himself, he knew it was only a mild flavour, and from past experience he didn't expect it to be anything that he could call exciting, though he hoped it would be.

He dipped his small tasting spoon into the custard and lifted it carefully to his lips, testing the temperature, to make sure it wasn't too hot to taste, and it wasn't. He dipped his spoon back into the pot collecting a full spoonful, then put it straight into his mouth.

Within 15 seconds he had tasted the milky custard, then the not so subtle taste of the beetroot. So far so good he thought. But the thought didn't last long as suddenly the full fury of the heat from the 'Everyday Seasoning' began to fill his mouth. Tariq started leaping around his shell wondering where he could get a jug of very cold water from, the extra seasoning had been too much and it had almost blown his tongue from his head with its fiery heat.

"Shell, Shell," he yelled, patting his mouth with his hands to no affect. "What am I going to do? How can I stop the fire?"

"I'm not sure," Shell said, smirking to herself. "You could try not putting beetroot in your custard next time," she added unhelpfully.

Tariq found a jug of his yet untested lettuce juice and gulped it down. The only thing he cared about at the moment was sorting out the fire that his tongue and mouth were now experiencing.

Although the juice was revolting it quelled his burning mouth and he was glad of that, but as soon as the fire had gone away he began to feel quite queasy. The lettuce juice had been something he had put aside many, many months ago and the skin he'd had to take from it, before he'd gulped it down, had wriggled with a life of its own, in his hands.

Chapter 36.
No More Buttons

Dave stopped pressing the buttons on the phone. He had finally got the better of the evil-doers. The electric Santa had stopped moving and everyone who had decided to take a Softy Mike toy, had dropped them, not wanting them any longer. This wasn't just because the toys were now burnt and charred globs of plastic lying on the floor, it was also because the RFID computer chips in them were fried and no longer sending out the mind controlling signals. Even the dastardly individuals behind the evil plan had disappeared. Dave was happy. Everything was sorted.

As Dave put, what he thought was the special mobile phone control unit, into one of his impossibly deep pockets, the Bobboggs, who had been watching the whole spectacle from the restaurant roof, leapt to the ground and made their way back into the forest. They had to find the man from the temple of Yoodoo so they could sing the story of Dave and the electric Santa, to let the shaman know exactly what had gone on. The Bobboggs were sure he would be happy to hear their song, even if it might be a little out of tune.

Dave brushed himself down and checked that the pink flower in his lapel could still be seen, even though it was a bit tatty. He knew that wearing the flower would show Tariq, if Tariq should ever turn up, that he was still around, and waiting. He settled on a seat next to the bar and ordered a fruit juice, one with umbrellas and swizzle sticks in, looking out for Tariq to appear.

Chapter 37.
Santa is Free

As Tariq's mouth began to get back to normal he wondered how his friend was doing. There was nothing going on in the apartment he was watching and he thought it was about time to seek out his friend. It had been two hours since he'd said goodbye to Dave, earlier that evening.

Tariq remembered what he'd been told and stuck a pink flower to his shell as he left the secluded position in the middle of the Hibiscus plant. He walked along the resort's paths past numerous chalets and apartments until he reached the resort's entertainment area. He looked towards the bar and noticed a bright pink tatty flower sticking out in the darkness of the rainy evening.

Tariq was relieved his friend was still around.

"Dave," he said as he approached. "What's going on?"

"Nothing now Tariq," Dave said, absolutely shattered.

"What about the evil-doers?" Tariq asked, not noticing any of the burning toys that littered the floor of the entertainment area.

"They're sorted."

"Don't tell me you've done it again," Tariq said.

"I'm sorry Tariq, but I can only tell you that I have — the evil-doers' plan has failed. There's only one problem though."

"What's that?"

"Santa is locked up!"

Tariq was surprised. Why on earth would Santa be locked up? He couldn't imagine. "Why's Santa locked up?"

"Because he isn't free," Dave replied. "I need to unlock the door to the storeroom. And there's some more bad news"

"What d'you mean bad news Dave?" Tariq asked, getting a little concerned.

"I don't know how we're going to get back home."

"Dave, don't forget the Yoodoo juice. We were told it would help if we believed in it; don't you remember?"

"Tariq, we're on the Island of Maiti, there are many superstitious beliefs and the fact that we have a flask of Yoodoo juice really means nothing; it's just about taking part in the culture, that's all. It's a nice flask though."

"That may be so Dave, but if we're going to take part shouldn't we at least let Santa out of the storeroom?"

The two friends walked over to the corridor behind the stage and unlocked the door to the storeroom, letting Santa out.

"Well, ho, ho, ho. Thank you my friends," Santa said as the door was opened.

"That's okay Santa, anything for you, anytime," Dave said, adding, "Don't know what we're going to do about this mess though." Dave pointed towards the burnt Softy Mikes and the mess the robot Santa had made of the stage and the entertainments area.

"Don't worry about that sonny," Santa said and as he did so, he waved his palm across the scene of upturned tables and broken sound systems, burnt teddies and broken glasses. In an instant there was a brief but bright burst of white light made from hundreds and thousands of pure white snowflakes, and everything became still and quiet. Even the sea seemed to stop making its slapping sounds against the beach. The black storm clouds above turned into a blanket of fluffy light-grey and the snowflakes began to settle on the ground.

Slowly but surely the broken furniture and equipment put itself back together and as the stage reconstructed, the snowflakes started to dissolve the remains of the toys and the robot. Finally, a white slatted door moved from where it was leaning and as it floated back to where it should be, it revealed a rather large Elf sitting on the floor and a small man with spectacles cowering behind him.

"Ho, ho, ho. There you are," Santa said.

The Elf that was, Gene Baubs and Gilbert Bates didn't move. They couldn't. Santa's magic had frozen them in place.

"I have some friends I would like you to meet," Santa said to the dastardly duo. And as he finished speaking the air became full of the sound of ringing sleigh bells. A hole opened up in the fluffy blanket of cloud high above the stage and through it came six reindeers pulling a large wooden sleigh. Within seconds the sleigh had come to a stop on the stage.

"I think it would be good if you two help me this Christmas," Santa said. "For all the trouble you have caused me. And you might learn a thing or two." He waved his hand at the cowering pair of evil-doers and they vanished in a puff of brilliant white snowflakes, reappearing in the sleigh looking very surprised, if not just a little bit worried as well.

Santa waved his hand over the sleigh and the reindeer shot off, back into the sky, towards the hole in the clouds, sleigh in tow. Seconds later the hole in the sky closed up and the sound of the sleigh bells began to fade away into the distance. After it had completely died away, the entertainments area of the resort completed its transformation back to normal. No sign of the mess remained and no sign that it had ever snowed on the Caribbean island of Maiti was to be seen. The thunder rumbled once again.

Dave frowned at the apparent magic, and then asked, "If you can do magic like that, Santa, why couldn't you stop what was going on?"

"That's very simple my dear Brave Dave. I cannot stop those who do wrong, but I can show them what is good, as I can only reward the good people of this world. In this way the wrong doers will eventually see that good things come only to those who do good themselves. There was a wise man in China I once knew, a very, very long time ago, his name was Confucius, and he told me one day, '*Do not treat others as you yourself would not be treated*' and he was quite right."

All Dave and Tariq could do was nod in agreement at the wise words.

"Ho, ho, ho," said Santa. "I think there is someone beckoning you." He pointed behind the two friends.

Dave and Tariq turned around to see one of the Bobboggs waving its arm at them, motioning for them to follow. Dave turned back to Santa to wish him well but the man in scarlet with fluffy white trimmings had disappeared.

Chapter 38.
End of the Holiday

Dave and Tariq followed the Bobbogg out of the Royal DeMacaroon Club Carib resort and into the jungle, along the loamy path they had taken the other day. The storm that had poured rain on the show had now done its bit for the environment and as they walked, the night sky became clear with the moon showing itself once again.

They followed the path and as they got deeper into the jungle a musical sound, from nowhere, gradually got louder. It was a sound of happy music, almost as if it was greeting them. It was not music played on electrical instruments but the music of bungle-bees and Bobboggs jamming together, elated by what had happened; the bungle-bees provided the rhythm and the Bobboggs sang the rest.

Bzzzzz, schtuma, bzzzzz, schtuma, bzzzzz, schtuma — hoo-hooo. It was almost a fanfare; a fanfare for them, Brave Dave and Tremendous Tariq. For the evil plan they had thwarted together.

Reaching the end of the track they recognised the Temple of Yoodoo, lit up by the light of many hundreds of candles, as it had been before. This time, standing outside it, was the shaman of Maiti in his brilliant bright-white robes, with arms open wide, welcoming them. Dave and Tariq came to a stop at the edge of the clearing.

"Welcom' mi manhole covers. Ya do great ahn good works for dis islan' a fi mi."

Dave shook his head. "It was nutten, jus' doin' mi corn on the cob. Seen?"

Tariq frowned and looked at Dave, wondering what on earth the shaman was saying.

"Gwaan," the shaman said laughing at Dave's modesty.

"A true," Dave said.

"A true, den," the shaman agreed. "'Ow a can 'elp ya, mi manhole covers?"

Dave, now that he had exhausted all of the lingo he had picked up on the island, said: "We need help to get back home."

"Yu hab de Yoodoo juice, Mon."

"Yes... but..."

"Here, here." The shaman said beckoning Tariq to take the flask out of his satchel. Tariq took it out and handed it over. The shaman then waved at two of the Bobboggs, who grabbed one of Dave and Tariq's hands each and led them to the largest coconut tree at the edge of the clearing, standing each of them on opposite sides and placing a large garland of bright flowers around their necks.

Dave looked at Tariq and shrugged his shoulders. Tariq shook his head. A Bobbogg who had been sitting high up in one of the Florida palms swung down from his perch on a vine, and then yanked it free from the canopy, handing it to the two Bobboggs that had led Tariq and Dave to the base of the coconut tree. Taking each end of the vine the two Bobboggs ran around and around the tree, waving their arms up and down as they did so, until Dave and Tariq were firmly attached to it; the vine having been wrapped around their waists, each of them with their back to the tree's trunk.

Next the shaman opened the top of the Yoodoo flask, dipped his hand in and started to flick the bananary honey smelling liquid on the tree's roots.

"So long," the shaman said, "and tanks for all de 'elp."

Tariq and Dave did not know what to make of the whole situation.

"Dave, what's going to happen?"

"Erm, I'm not quite sure," he replied. "But I think we're going."

"How d'you know that?"

"The man said 'so long'."

"Ah! Of course. But how are we going anywhere like this?" Tariq said.

Before Dave could answer the base of the tree started to fizz; yellow, green and red puffs of smoke came from its roots as the whole trunk started to shake.

"So long mi manhole covers. One love."

As soon as the shaman had finished speaking the coconut tree lifted into the air, hovering for just a few seconds.

"Bye then," Dave said.

"Yeah, bye then," Tariq stammered in agreement.

There was a massive boom and the coconut tree, with Tariq and Dave attached, blasted off into the sky.

"Whooooa," both Dave and Tariq yelled as the wind began to whistle past their ears.

Quickly the small Island of Maiti became ever smaller as Tariq and Dave watched it disappear beneath them, becoming just a small dot in a huge ocean of night blue sea. The world beneath them passed in a blur and the night became brighter and more like daylight as they travelled.

"LOOK TARIQ, THAT'S ENGLAND," Dave yelled against the wind, as he recognised the land they were now aiming for.

"IS THAT GOOD DAVE?" Tariq yelled back.

"I THINK SO."

"ONLY THINK SO?" Tariq yelled, astounded by Dave's apparent lack of concern.

Suddenly the coconut tree started moving towards the ground and Tariq had a feeling of déjà vu come over him. He knew what it was like to be many thousands of feet above the ground without any adequate way to stop the inevitable crunch when they reached it.

"YOU'VE DONE IT AGAIN DAVE," Tariq yelled, against the noisy and whistling wind.

"DONE WHAT?"

"DOESN'T MATTER."

The tree continued its descent.

"LOOK, THERE'S YOUR HUTCH TARIQ," Dave said, as he recognised the garden they were now heading towards at an extremely fast speed.

"GREAT! WILL IT HURT?"

"AT THIS SPEED, I THINK, VERY PROBABLY," Dave replied.

"TREMENDOUS."

"WAIT A MINUTE."

"I CAN'T. HOW CAN I POSSIBLY WAIT WHEN I'M ATTACHED TO A COCONUT TREE TRAVELLING AT WHO KNOWS WHAT SPEED, TOWARDS THE GROUND? IT'S BEYOND MY CAPABILITIES."

"I THINK," Dave began, then lowered his voice as the wind started to die away, "the tree is slowing down."

The tree rotated in the air so that its base was now downwards, as if it was going to land.

"I don't believe it," Tariq said.

The tree's roots splodged down into the mud at the end of Tariq's pen and stopped. The vine that had kept Tariq and Dave attached to the coconut tree for their entire journey unravelled itself and they both fell face first into the gooey mud.

Chapter 39.
Back Home

Tariq and Dave picked themselves out of the mud and stepped away from the large coconut tree just in time to miss being crushed by it as it fell over, splashing and sinking beneath the mud of Tariq's pen.

"I think we deserve a cup of tea," Tariq said, glancing back at the disappearing coconut trunk. "That was quite a close call."

"Tariq, I think you're right. This whole holiday has been a lot more exhausting than I thought it was going to be."

The two travellers splodged their way up Tariq's pen towards his hutch, their feet making sucking sounds with each step they made. Eventually they were standing outside Tariq's front door and before entering they brushed themselves down removing all the mud they could, especially from their brightly coloured floral garlands.

Once inside Tariq put the kettle on and they both collapsed onto Tariq's sofa, utterly worn out.

"An interesting holiday, Dave," Tariq observed.

"Yeah. It certainly was."

"But next time, if there is one, I DO NOT WANT TO BE DROPPED FROM THE SKY," Tariq stated in the firmest manner he could muster. "IT'S NOT NICE."

"Okay Tariq, Okay. It won't happen again — unless it's really necessary."

Tariq didn't make any further comment because he knew, if Dave got a feeling that they would be needed somewhere, to help any needful people, he wouldn't be able to say no. Not even if it meant flying again.

*

The next few days passed without incident and the friends relaxed in the warmth of Tariq's hutch but just as they were getting used to the peacefulness of their after holiday break, a loud noise started up; something had triggered Tariq's S.C.A.R.P.A system.

Yet again Dave was thrown from the sofa he was resting on as the lights in the hutch went out.

"Dave, it's the Land Lords. Act like a feather," Tariq said, as he disappeared into his shell.

Dave laid flat on the floor of the hutch pretending to be a feather, which wasn't too difficult.

The roof of the hutch opened up and John Jones looked in, Maddy and Jim had been insistent that he checked to make sure their tortoise was okay. As John looked around the inside of the hutch, he frowned. Somehow, during their holiday in Jamaica, the tortoise had found a floral garland and had put it on and, not only that, the feather he'd seen in the hutch before he'd taken his family on holiday, had also gained a floral garland.

John placed his hand gently on the tortoise's shell to feel if it was still warm, and then smiled. The tortoise was definitely warm and this meant it was still alive, as he knew it would be.

Closing the roof of the hutch he wondered for a moment about the garlands then dismissed the thought. The tortoise was okay and there was no bad news to tell his children. He made his way back up the garden into the house through the kitchen to tell Maddy and Jim the good news.

About the Author

After working consistently in I.T. for 27 years I decided it was time to forego the strictly logical world of computing and take up writing in my spare time. I don't think I'll ever truly get to grips with this literary world but I'm certainly having great fun finding out about it, though I think my wife, Yve, is not so enamoured by my frequent requests asking 'what do you think of this?'

That said, without her, I don't think my three

children's books would have ever seen the light of day and I wouldn't have enough stuff to be able to have my very own website created — www.srwoodward.co.uk.

Other Brave Dave books;

Brave Dave; The Makings of a Hero

Brave Dave and The Time Goblin

Coming very, very soon;

Brave Dave and The Space Oddity

www.BraveDave.co.uk

www.srwoodward.co.uk

Proof

Made in the USA
Charleston, SC
19 October 2014